BEST LESBIAN
ROMANCE
2010

BEST LESBIAN ROMANCE 2010

EDITED BY
RADCLYFFE

CLEIS
PRESS

Published in the United States.
Cleis Press Inc., P.O. Box 14697, San Francisco, California 94114.

Printed in the United States.
Cover design: Scott Idleman
Cover photograph: Hans Neleman/Getty Images
Text design: Frank Wiedemann
Cleis logo art: Juana Alicia
First Edition.
10 9 8 7 6 5 4 3 2 1

ISBN 13: 978-1-57344-376-0

"Queens Up" © Andrea Dale appeared in *Lesbian Cowboys: Erotic Adventures* (Cleis Press, 2009); "The Outside Edge" © Sacchi Green appeared in *Girl Crazy* (Cleis Press, 2009); "Soaked" © Erin O'Riordan appeared in *Sinister Wisdom* (2009); "All In" © Radclyffe appeared in *In Deep Waters 2: Cruising the Strip* (Bold Strokes Books, 2008); "Girls and Their Cars" © Renée Strider appeared in *Girl Crazy* (Cleis Press, 2009).

Contents

I INTRODUCTION

Love is one of those rare experiences that engage us on every plane—the mind, the heart, the spirit, and the body. The totality and intensity of the sensation probably explains why love and romance are such powerful drivers in our lives, urging us to connect deeply and intimately with others without reservation. Love has been likened to psychosis, albeit mostly a pleasant one—making us forgo our ordinary caution and rationality, sometimes risking heartbreak and disappointment, in order to share our deepest selves. Romance is the vehicle of that insanity—seducing us, amazing us, and in the best of times, freeing us to become more than we have ever been before. As with love, the nature of romance changes as we change—as we risk, as we lose, as we grow, as we triumph.

The stories selected for this anthology are as varied as our unique and irreproducible experiences of falling in love, of being in love, and of remaining in love—for a moment or a lifetime—and as universal as the commonality that we as lesbians recognize in our struggles and our victories to love who and how we choose. Anna Meadows's "Coming Out Party" and Erin O'Riordan's "Soaked" capture the wild exuberance and agonies of young passion; Dalia Craig's "The Last Dance" assures us that what begins in a moment of insuppressible desire may indeed prove to be the substance of a lifetime if we are brave enough to embark on the adventure. Sometimes we take that chance and lose, but Cheyenne Blue's "Five" and Kris Adams's "Hard to Hate Her," remind us that we can emerge from disappointment and broken dreams stronger, braver, and able to embrace the wonder of love again. As in Jacqueline Applebee's "I Never Thought of Love," the relationships that change our lives don't always arrive with fanfare, but sneak up on us, becoming so much a part of the daily landscape of our existence that our lives are changed forever almost without our knowing. Whether recounting the headlong fall into love at first glance or the subtle force of fate and circumstance that leads us to see the true nature of love in a different light, as with the two competitors in Renée Strider's "Girls and Their Cars," the stories in this anthology celebrate the joy, the diversity, and the passion of lesbian love in all its many wondrous forms.

Radclyffe

WHEN WE ALMOST MET

Evan Mora

We almost met in 1993, and again in 1998. We might have met on campus, or later, in a bar; we could have met just walking down the street. It would be eight more years before we found each other, but I believe we've crossed paths many times before, we two. Sam and I.

In the fall of 1993 I was eighteen years old, a freshman in university, wide-eyed and naive, transplanted from my hometown of nine hundred to a city of three million, and a university of forty thousand. Daunting to say the least.

"Do you want us to stay?" my parents asked when the boxes had been unloaded, and I was terrified at the thought of being alone in the sea of strangers that moved around us.

"No," I replied, my resolve marginally stronger than my fear. "I'm good."

So many new faces, so much to learn, so many discoveries yet to make. I played a lot of sports, made good grades, snuck my way into too many bars, and dated some forgettable guy.

In the fall of 1993 Sam was twenty-three. She was in her last year of law school, living with her girlfriend right around the corner from my dorm. She did volunteer work for a legal aid clinic on campus, worried about paying the bills, and fell asleep every night in the arms of someone she loved.

I spent a lot of time in the law library; I imagine that she did too.

One of my roommates really wanted to get into law school. We studied in the law library because she said it inspired her. I went along because it was quieter than the dorm, and less congested than the main campus library.

How many times were we there together, I wonder? Did we spend an afternoon side by side, immersed in our respective texts? Or did we, perhaps, cross paths at the door—she on her way in and me on my way out? I wonder if our eyes ever met. What would she have seen in the fresh-faced country girl I was then? Would her heart have tripped just a little, the way it did all those years later? Would I have felt that telltale fluttering in my stomach? The one that told me I was in trouble the minute she said *hello*? Maybe.

But she was in love, and I had that guy.... I'd never kissed a girl, and she was already trying to build a future. We couldn't have met then, could we? No. We weren't ready yet.

In the summer of 1998 I was twenty-three. I had a good job with even better hours—perfect for endless summer nights at the bars. I loved the atmosphere, loved the heat and the smoke and the heavy beat of the music. I was in love with loving women, and in love with the game. A shared glance across a crowded room, tentative smiles and shy flirtation, the delicious feel of two bodies moving sensuously together on the dance floor. I'd been with a woman or two—people I'd met through work—but that summer was definitely my first season in queer society. I felt more at home in my skin than I'd ever felt in my life.

In the summer of 1998 Sam was twenty-eight. She was a hotshot young lawyer with the world at her fingertips. She worked hard and played harder. She calls that summer her "summer of disrepute"—and from anything I've ever heard, the name fit. The stories say she could make a girl cross the length of the room with no more than a gesture. She'd leave her friends shaking their heads as she tossed a smile over her shoulder on the way to the door, arm thrown casually around the shoulder of her newfound companion. No one ever asked her if she remembered their names.

I don't know how we *didn't* meet that summer. Seems impossible, really.

With her short dark hair falling casually across her forehead, already streaked with the silver that draws me like a magnet, there's no question that she would have caught my eye. I'm fairly certain I would have caught hers too.

What might have happened, had our eyes met then?

I would have smiled at her, I'm sure. I might have looked down for a heartbeat, but there's no doubt I would have looked again, a coy smile playing at the corners of my mouth. She would have been smiling that cocky, self-assured smile I know so well—the one that screams sex appeal, and really, well...I would have been lost.

She would have gestured for me to come, and I would have mimed a little *Who, me?* back to her. She would have nodded and I would have paused, pretending to consider what required no consideration at all before slowly making my way to her side.

She would have given me some bad line, and I would have laughed at how terrible it sounded...but I still would have let her buy me a drink. I imagine standing there by the bar, swirling the ice cubes in my glass while she toyed with the label on her bottle, making the kind of small talk that strangers make when the undercurrent of electricity has sparked between them, but has yet to be acknowledged outright.

"I haven't seen you here before," she would have said.

"Oh, I don't know," I might have replied, "there are so many women here, it's hard to keep track of all the faces...."

"A lot of faces, sure," she'd have continued, "but none as pretty as yours."

It's the kind of line that should come off sounding heavy-handed and insincere, but looking into the handsome face of the smooth, well-dressed butch she would have been then, her dark eyes promising all kinds of heaven, I would have eaten it up like candy.

"Dance with me?" she would have said, hand outstretched to take my own. She would have phrased it like a question, but only to be polite.

I would have slipped my hand into hers and followed her into the rich heated darkness of the dance floor, would have welcomed her hands at my waist, drawing me firmly against her frame. My hand would have traveled up her forearm, over bicep and shoulder, would have come to rest against the soft skin of her nape.

Her dark eyes would have glittered with approval, would have caught and held mine as our bodies moved together in rhythm with the music. It's a seduction all its own, dancing with Sam—the slow grind of her body into mine, one hand reaching up, the pad of her thumb stroking across my lower lip, the other hand sliding lower, splayed wide just above the curve of my backside, pressing me closer, her thigh between mine, a prelude of intimacies to come.

She would have kissed me then, a deceptive kiss with gentle beginnings, teasing the corners of my mouth with soft feathery touches. My mouth would have opened beneath hers, an invitation for more that she would have gladly taken. Her mouth would have fused hungrily to mine, her fist bunching in my hair, her tongue stroking deeply against my own.

"Come home with me," she would have said. An offer I could not have refused.

But we were both dangerous that summer, in our own particular ways. She was nursing a broken heart, mourning the loss of that incredible first love—the one that we always think will last forever. And me? I wanted nothing but fun, because my heart belonged to someone else—someone who couldn't be with me, but who, from time to time, pretended she was. So we couldn't have met then either, not really.

How long does it take to heal a broken heart? How long does it take to recover from that kind of intense, soul-deep young love? There's no timeline to follow, no set course to take. We each do what we need to do. We mature. We move on. We live our lives.

Sam met someone new, and so did I. Over the next eight years our lives had many parallels, though our paths never crossed. She was happy, and so was I. We each did well in our life—enjoyed our share of successes and travels, the company of friends and the security of home.

But every heart yearns for the one that completes it, for the one that inspires it and makes it feel free. Every heart wants the one that makes it beat faster, makes it overflow with uncontainable joy. Without it there's a loneliness that can't quite be defined, a quiet despair that never quite goes away.

And so it was with Sam and me, both single again, both

hopeless romantics in search of that intangible *something*, living our lives ignorant of each other. Then a chance meeting—a fluke—one in a million, changed both of our lives forever. Luck? Happenstance? Call it whatever you like. All these years and all these places we could have, *should* have met, but didn't...and then one day, fate sits us down side by side on a train.

I hadn't traveled by train in years. I'm not entirely sure why I did that particular time either. I made my way down the aisle, ticket in hand, and stopped when I reached my seat. There was someone in it, lost in thought, staring unseeingly out the window. I appraised the would-be seat thief for a moment before I spoke and felt a faint stir of interest.

"Hello?" I said to attract her attention.

"Hello," she returned, her eyes now on mine.

"I think you're in my seat?" I gestured to the window seat she was occupying with the ticket in my hand.

"You're right, I'm sorry." She offered a sheepish smile, which did funny things to my insides. "I thought it might have been empty, and I'd just switch spots to enjoy the view." She stood up and moved into the aisle so that I could take my seat, so close I could smell the subtle fragrance of her cologne.

"Sometimes you get lucky," I offered philosophically.

"Yes," she replied with a pause, "sometimes you do."

We talked for five hours. About everything. About nothing. We talked with the intimacy of strangers, with the fevered intensity that arises when like minds meet. There wasn't a moment of awkward silence, and somewhere in the middle of excited exclamations of *I know how you feel,* and *Yes—I know exactly what you mean!* I became fixated on her mouth, wondering what it would feel like pressed against mine, wanting it more than I could remember wanting anything in a very long time.

As daylight faded and the miles flew past, the atmosphere

between us changed ever so slightly. The ride was almost over. She had a difficult trial beginning in a couple of days; I was visiting an aunt who'd recently moved to this city. She'd be there for three weeks, while I was heading home in a few days. We traded numbers with promises to meet again when we were both back home, but I couldn't help but feel like I was losing something I'd only just found.

Exiting the train station, I saw my aunt waving excitedly, and nearby, a driver holding a sign with Sam's name on it. We stopped for a moment to say our good-byes, and she wrapped me in a warm embrace. Being pressed close to her like that in the middle of all those people was a particular kind of torture, sweet and arousing all at the same time. And if she held me a little tighter, and the brush of her lips against my cheek lingered a little longer than was customary between two strangers like we were, no one was the wiser.

She called me that night.

In fact, she called me every night for the next three weeks. Sometimes we only spoke for a few minutes.

"I missed the sound of your voice," she'd say.

Sometimes we talked for hours, late into the night, like crazy teenagers who never run out of things to say. I became intimately acquainted with all the nuances of her voice. How it took on a bit of a husky edge when she was tired, how there was an underlying edge of strain in it at the end of a particularly trying day in court. I loved the way her voice became a low sensuous growl when we'd exhausted polite conversation and found ourselves discussing much more personal pleasures and desires. She sent shivers down my spine.

We'd made a date for the night of her return, dinner at a nice place downtown. It seemed funny, calling it a first date, when really I felt like I'd known her forever. I *was* nervous though,

I'll admit that. I spent more time than I needed to getting ready, selecting and then discarding half the contents of my wardrobe before I settled on a simple green cashmere sweater and my favorite pair of jeans. It wasn't my appearance I was worried about though, not really.

The simple fact was, we'd only spent those few hours on the train together and had shared only that one too brief hug. I felt like I knew her intimately—we'd shared so many of our secrets and fears and wants and desires—but what if none of that translated into tangible chemistry?

My thoughts were interrupted by the chime of the doorbell. She'd arrived. My stomach was filled with a thousand butterflies as I crossed the room and opened the door. She stood beneath my porch light in a faded leather jacket, hands buried in her pockets to stave off the winter night's chill.

"Hi…" I said—it seemed all I could manage. I hadn't done justice to her in my memory. Her eyes were a richer, darker color than I'd remembered, and her mouth was more full and sensuous.

"Hi." She smiled, which made the butterflies go crazy.

"Do you want to come in?" I opened the door wider. She nodded without speaking and stepped past me into the house. She was taller than I'd remembered too, I realized as she closed the distance between us. She had yet to take off her coat, and I'd barely closed the door when her hands framed my face and her mouth hungrily found mine.

There was no hesitation in her touch, in her kiss. There were no gentle explorations or soft whispered words. There was only burning need—both hers and mine—consuming us with an intensity that bordered on desperation.

I'd worried about chemistry, but this was so much more. Kissing Sam was like…coming home, and I didn't think I could ever get enough. She kicked off her shoes and we fumbled with her jacket, her mouth never once leaving mine. We took a couple of steps, in no particular direction, and I bumped up against the kitchen counter. Without missing a beat, her hands were at my waist, lifting me so that I was sitting atop it, and she was positioned firmly between my thighs. I moaned at the contact, which inflamed her all the more, one hand tightening at my waist, the other burying itself in the length of my hair.

I don't know how long we stayed like that, ten minutes? Twenty minutes? Thirty? I only know that at some point the terrible desperate need eased a little, and we could pause for a moment, even smile a little, and offer small soothing kisses to swollen lips.

I think we knew then that we were at some great beginning. I felt it, and I could see it in her eyes. And it's weird, but knowing that made me suddenly feel as though we had all the time in the world, for everything.

I hopped off the counter and took her by the hand, leading her up the stairs and into my room. She sat on the edge of my bed and I stood before her, removing my clothes until I was fully revealed. For a moment she said nothing, but her eyes were alight with desire, moving over my body in an intimate caress that aroused me more than anything else she might have done.

"You're beautiful," was all she said, and she held her hand out for mine, pulling me gently toward her and into her lap so that I was cradled against her chest.

She kissed me again, slowly this time, with a devastating thoroughness that left me breathless. And while her mouth was exploring mine, her hands were discovering new territory as well. Her palm smoothed over the contour of my hip, spanned the curve of my belly, traced the bottom of my rib cage. There was possession in her touch when her hand cupped my breast, teasing my nipple into aching hardness.

I moaned against her mouth, a pleading sound, needing more.

"Spread your legs," she whispered against my jaw, her mouth trailing kisses along its length, her tongue teasing my ear, her teeth nipping the tender skin beneath.

I did as she asked and felt, more than heard, her low sound of approval. Her fingers traced lightly over my heated flesh, dipped teasingly into the moisture they found. She did this again, and then once more, her mouth all the while continuing to wreak havoc on the sensitive column of my neck. I couldn't keep still, even had I wanted to. My hands roamed restlessly across her shoulders and through her hair, my hips rose off her lap of their own accord, trying desperately to follow the move-ment of her hand.

"Sam, please," I begged, "I need you."

She pressed her forehead against my shoulder, a helpless shudder running through her at my words. Her mouth reached blindly for mine, this kiss harder and more aggressive than the ones before. Her tongue stroked deeply into my mouth as her fingers thrust into me. My body was on fire, a fine sheen of perspiration coating my skin as she loved me like that. Her thumb stroked my clit each time she thrust, her mouth kissing me everywhere she could reach. I shuddered as I came, crying out against her shoulder, feeling her heart beating beneath my cheek every bit as fast as my own. She rocked me for a while, until my skin cooled and our breathing slowed, then she urged me beneath the covers, removing her clothes to join me.

We never did make it to the restaurant that night—we had too much lost time to make up for. We still shake our heads about all the parallels in our lives, about all the times we almost but didn't quite meet. Sometimes I can't help but wonder what our lives would have been like if we'd met all those years ago, and I feel a twinge of sadness thinking about the time we've missed. But who knows? We were different people back then. Maybe we'd have met and then gone our separate ways, never recognizing in each other the very thing we were searching for. We couldn't have met back then. We couldn't have met until we did. Until we were ready for forever.

COMING OUT PARTY

Anna Meadows

The first trouble came with deciding the name they would announce when I took my St. James's bow.

"Jacqueline" is a big name on my dad's side of the family, so my mom never loved the fact that I shortened it. But it wasn't my fault. In the first grade, we Jacquelines realized there were four of us running around, each coming to answer our shared name whenever a TA called it. The four of us doesn't even include Jacqueline Jane Hulburd, who had been calling herself JJ since preschool and wouldn't answer to anything else.

Jacqueline Melody Morris volunteered to go by her middle name in exchange for first pick from the jump rope bucket at recess. That left the rest of us to play rock-paper-scissors to decide who was gonna be called what. Jacqueline Aarons got the first pick, so she got "Jackie." Jacqueline Young won the next game, and went with the full thing. That left me.

Jackie and Jacqueline would have just skipped off to get in line for the tetherball court, but they knew my new brother was in the hospital. So they dragged the toes of their jellies over the blacktop and suggested "Quelly" or "Lin," but I didn't like either, so I became plain old Jack, and I've been plain old Jack ever since.

"I can assure you, none of the other debutantes will be announced by a nickname!"

Whenever my mother said a sentence with the word *debutante* in it, I imagined her jaw loosening to a Southern drawl, her hair lightening and growing larger as she spoke.

I always thought I'd have a sweet sixteen at the Acapulco Restaurant. I had never heard of a teenage girl in a big white dress for any other reason than a shotgun wedding. But it all made my mom so happy, and I couldn't think of a good reason to turn down shopping for the prettiest, puffiest ball gown we could find.

Puffy, because Angela Aarons, president of the League of Mother-Daughter Philanthropists, told our mothers that if each of us didn't look like a frosted cupcake the moment we bowed, they had failed. So my mom helped me on and off with a half-dozen dresses at the Bridal Barn while old ladies clucked about how young I was and looked over the edges of their glasses to see if my stomach was rounded under the bodice of the dress.

On the seventh my mother stood back and pressed her hands together. "Oh."

This was never a good sign. She only ever put her hands together without closing her eyes when she was about to cry or yell.

I swished the skirt. "You like it?"

"You are a vision. A vision."

I twirled in the mirror. "Can we afford it?"

"Hush, Jacqueline." She looked around the store. "Let me worry about that. And you'll take Alexander to get measured for his tux tomorrow?"

"Of course. I told you I would." I lifted my elbows away from the bodice of the dress so the fabric rosettes would stop rubbing the undersides of my upper arms. "Why isn't he here now?"

"He's working on a school project at Tommy's house. They're doing a presentation on…" She snapped her fingers as she thought. "Nuclear fission?"

"What's that?"

She billowed the skirt from the hem. "I don't know. I leave it to him."

Al stood in front of the junior high with a huge Styrofoam ball tucked under his arm, the surface spray-painted as teal as Mom's car.

"What the hell is that?" I asked.

He set it on his lap and slammed the door. "It's *going* to be a model of a boron atom. I just need to carve out a spot for a nucleus in the electron cloud."

"If that thing gets little bits of foam all over Mom's car, I'm not cleaning it up." I pulled onto the highway. "What are you smirking about? Nuclear fission?"

"I know a secret."

"Yeah. I bet you know all kinds of secrets about the periodic table, Galileo."

"He was an astronomer."

"I don't care."

He kept grinning.

"I don't care," I said. "I really don't."

"Okay."

"I don't."

"Sure."

I pulled one of Mom's Camels out of the ashtray, her lipstick still printed around the filter, and lit the end. She always put out cigarettes when they were at least half an inch from being done.

"That's gross," said Al.

"It's economical." I took a drag and tucked the cigarette between my third and fourth fingers as I drove. "All right, fine. What is it?"

"What's what?"

"Your secret."

"I thought you didn't care."

"I don't. But I'm bored."

He hugged the boron atom against his chest and didn't talk until we got off the highway and approached the mall. "You have someone who likes you."

"Oh, big deal. Everyone has someone who likes them. Even you." I reached over and ruffled his hair. "Who is it?"

"Why should I tell you? You don't even care."

"All right, I care. You happy?"

He beamed. "Yes. Very."

"Now who is it?"

He leaned over the middle seat and snatched Mom's cigarette out of my hand.

"Hey!"

He threw it out the window. "He thinks it's gross when you smoke."

As we were walking through the Bridal Barn parking lot, Al stopped and looked at me. "You're really not gonna grow anymore, are you?"

"Gee, thanks." I walked toward the door.

He followed me. "I didn't mean it in a mean way. I'm just saying. You haven't had to get a bigger shoe size in two years. Orthopedically speaking, that pretty much means you're done."

I rolled my eyes and opened the shop door. "I appreciate the diagnosis, Dr. Montgomery."

"Don't sweat it." He set his elbow on my shoulder, something he had loved doing ever since he passed me on the kitchen door height chart. "Besides, he likes that you're short."

I groaned.

"He also knows you're not a natural blonde."

"Yeah, who doesn't?" I stopped in front of the glass-topped desk. "Hi." I squinted to see the name tag gleaming against the woman's cream blazer. "I need a tux for my little brother." I elbowed him. "The appointment's under Montgomery."

The woman scanned the calendar with her finger. "Ah. Here you are. Alexander Montgomery."

He grimaced. "It's Al."

"He's only Alexander on his report card."

"I see." The woman smiled. "Right this way, sir. Go ahead and take a seat, Miss Montgomery. We'll have him measured in just a few minutes."

I flopped down in one of the chairs in the waiting area, the burnt-out velvet worn darker and thin. I was pretty sure they had been there since the Bridal Barn opened. I had rubbed my palms over the fuzzed fabric when my mother was picking up my flower-girl dress for Aunt Julie's wedding.

Bobbie crossed the lobby toward the door, the hanger of her rental tux hooked onto her fingers. I sunk down farther in the chair and wondered if I could duck behind the veil display without her noticing.

She stopped in front of me. "Hiding?"

I sat up straight. "I'm surrounded by miles of silk chiffon. You gotta be ready for anything."

She smiled. "Don't I know it."

"Your mom isn't getting you into a dress for this one?"

"What do you think?"

I smoothed my skirt. "Good thing you're tall. Or else you'd look like a ring bearer with that thing."

"Watch it. I was a ring bearer once."

I bit my lip, my teeth pulling off flecks of dry skin. Every fall, when the winds kicked up, my lips got so chapped I could hear it when I rubbed them together. I looked down at the floral rug that spanned the width of the lobby.

Bobbie nodded. "Take care, Jack."

I pulled my knees up onto the chair and looked out through the white script lettering on the plate glass storefront. Bobbie crossed the parking lot, the garment bag slung over her shoulder, her shoes kicking up dust from the ground that lightened the bottoms of her jeans. She had cut her hair again, a couple of weeks earlier. It didn't fall in her eyes or brush the tops of her ears anymore.

"Earth to sister?"

I jumped and turned around. "God."

"Yes, my child?"

I rolled my eyes. "You done?"

Al nodded. "They now know every measurement I have."

I pushed on the arms of the chair to get up. "Come on."

Al sat the atom model in the back seat and buckled the shoulder belt over it.

"You're kidding right?"

He slid into the passenger seat. "You drive like Grandma."

"I do not."

"Then why'd it take you five tries to get your license?"

"Four, smart-ass." I pulled his seat belt out of the socket and put the buckle in his hand.

"That was him by the way."

"Who was who?"

He clicked the buckle. "The guy you were talking to."

"Which guy?"

"Bobbie Slezak. That's the guy who likes you."

"That's a girl, genius."

"Then why is he renting a tux?"

"She dresses like a guy."

"Well, if it walks like a duck and it talks like a duck..."

"More like a dyke."

"I'm gonna tell Dad you said that word."

"Go ahead." I started the engine and backed out of the parking space. "Mom and her charity buddies use it all the time. Who told you she liked me anyway?"

"Libby Williams. She heard from her big sister that Bobbie's been staring at you in class all the time."

"Well, Libby Williams only said that because she probably likes *you*. She didn't even know Bobbie's a girl. I think we call that uninformed scientific data."

"Why don't you have her be your escort instead of me?" asked Al.

"Because she's a girl, stupid. Girls can't escort girls."

"Why not?" he asked.

"They just can't."

"Isn't there someone else you want to be your escort more than me?"

I bit my lip and thought of the boys in my class, their complexions reddened from the alcohol of aftershave and drinking too much sugary soda. "Nope. Sorry. You're the handsomest this town has to offer."

"God help the future of the race."

"Hey. Don't put down the Montgomery gene pool."

"Don't use the word *dyke*."

I groaned.

"You shouldn't say *shit* either." He sat up straight and put his hand to his chest. "It's unbecoming of a debutante."

I shoved his shoulder. "Fuck you." I stopped the car when we caught up with Bobbie. I rolled down the window. "Get in, Slezak."

She shrugged and opened the back door. "Thanks." She stared across the seat at the model. "And who's this?"

"A future Boron model," said Al.

Bobbie nodded. "Cool."

Al looked back at her. "It's not finished."

"What's missing?"

"Um, a nucleus," said Al.

"Gotcha," said Bobbie.

I pulled off the highway into town. "Al, where am I taking you?"

"Library. I'm meeting someone there."

"Who, Libby Williams?"

Al glared at me.

I stopped in front of the library. "Mom wants to know if you'll be gracing us with your presence at dinner."

"Yeah."

"Don't forget your baby," I said.

Al unbuckled the atom model. "Yeah, what did you ever build? A human pyramid?"

I looked back at Bobbie. "Hiding?"

She laughed and got in the front seat.

"So your mom roped you into going?"

"Yes."

I reached back and touched the rental bag. "She know you're wearing a tux?"

"Yep. That was part of the deal. The offspring of the decorating committee chair can't be a no-show."

"Who're you taking?"

"I think I'm going stag," she said. "Who's taking you?"

"Oh, he's a real charmer."

"Yeah?"

"Good looking. Brainy. And probably at the reference desk as we speak."

She smiled. "Brotherly love?"

"You got a better idea?"

"No. But doesn't he?"

"There's a reason he doesn't have curfew this week. You're not the only one making deals."

She nodded. "Nice. Nice."

"You taking Lauren in..." I counted on my fingers. "Five years?"

"I don't think they'd let me."

"True. Your cummerbund alone will be a scandal."

I pulled back onto the highway and parked across from the gas station. The trees on the sides of the road had shed leaves onto the pavement, cars kicking up the burnt orange whenever they sped past.

Bobbie looked out into the trees. "This definitely isn't my neighborhood."

I swallowed.

"Jack?"

I grabbed her shirt collar and kissed her, her Chapstick gliding over my mouth. She wrapped her arms around my waist and pulled me into the passenger seat. I picked up the clean, cotton scent on her skin and clothes, the smell I used to think was the soap she used.

She pulled away enough to look at me. "So." She squinted. She was farsighted. "We on again?"

I buried my hands in her hair. "Do we have to talk about that right now?"

"I think it's a good idea. Considering what happened last time."

I kissed her neck. "Why does that matter?"

She breathed in. "Well, I'm not really looking forward to getting dumped again."

"I didn't dump you."

"What did you do then?"

"You were talking to me. At school."

"Right. We were just talking. Not doing this. On the quad. It's not like anyone could have figured it out."

"Yeah, but everyone knows." I slipped my fingers between her belt and her jeans. "About you."

"You were talking to a dyke." She put her hand on mine and held my fingers still. "Big deal. It's not contagious, you know."

"Guilt by association." I kissed her cheek.

"It's not a crime either. At least not in this state."

I pulled the end of her belt out of the belt loop with my other hand. "You gonna talk through this whole thing, Slezak?"

She looked down at my fingers. "No." She slid her hand onto the back of my neck and pulled me closer to her.

I guided her palm to the front of my thigh and closed my eyes, to the leaves like cabbage moths, to the evergreens and the darkening blue of the sky, until there was nothing but the scent of fabric softener and the heat of Bobbie's fingertips on the fullest point of my hips.

I finger-combed my hair and opened the back door.

Al sat at the kitchen table and flipped the page of his *Scientific American*. "Looks good on you."

I stopped. "What?"

"The walk of shame."

"Screw you." I poured a glass from the carton of skim milk. Al looked across the kitchen. "I refuse to drink that stuff."

"Yeah, well Mom's not gonna buy two-percent again until after the ball, so get used to it."

"I guess I could reduce it on the stove...." He stroked his chin with his thumb and forefinger. "Why must we all suffer just because she's dieting?"

"It's not just her." I put the blue carton back in the door. "She says I look like I've put on a little weight." I looked down at my stomach. "You know, just around the waist and thighs."

"Even if you had, your dress is thicker than a Mylar vest. Nobody's gonna see anything except your head and arms."

"Mom says I have good arms."

"Well then you can die happy, can't you?"

I looked out the kitchen window into the empty driveway. "Where are they anyway?"

"They went to the store. We're out of lettuce."

"God forbid."

"My sentiments exactly," said Al.

I stood on my toes so I could see out into the street. "How long you think until they get back?"

"No, you don't have time to cross town for another round if that's what you mean."

"I don't know what you're talking about." I dropped a couple of ice cubes into my milk. "I was just gonna practice doing my hair."

Al shuddered. "How can you do that? It's like drinking cloudy water."

"I like it with ice. It tastes better."

"Nonfat milk's already watered down. You're just taking something that has little nutritional value and making it have no nutritional value whatsoever."

I finished the glass and grabbed my book bag. "So it's like the food equivalent of hearing you talk?"

Al smiled. "Touché, Sis." He flipped the pages open to another article. "Maybe there's still hope for you."

Bobbie's mother opened the door and lifted an eyebrow so neatly tweezed it looked drawn on.

"Hi, Mrs. Slezak." Before I realized it I had lifted onto the balls of my feet. I had forgotten that flats were never a good idea around Bobbie's house. Even her little sister had three inches on me. "I'm just here to return a book I borrowed from Bobbie."

"Uh-huh." She pursed the matte magenta of her lips together and held the door open wider. "You know the way."

I stopped at the top of the stairs. "Hi."

Bobbie got up from her desk.

I stepped into the doorway of her room. "I just came to return your book."

She squinted at the cover. "The History of the North American Audubon Society?"

I pushed the door shut behind me and kissed her so hard she stumbled back.

"You gotta quit this, Jack."

I wrapped my arms around her shoulders. "Like you mind."

"I just need to know where I stand."

I put a hand between her breasts. "You shouldn't be standing anywhere." I pushed her down onto her bed and climbed on top of her, our weight wrinkling her bedspread into darker green folds.

She crawled out from under me and sat up. "Look, I can't just do this with you. I can't just have sex when you feel like it and ignore you when you don't."

"I never said you had to ignore me."

"You kinda did." She scooted to the edge of the bed and put her feet on the floor. "You didn't even look at me at school."

I shrugged. "I'm here now."

"Yeah, and you'll be here as long as you want it. And as soon as you're not feeling amorous anymore, I'm out in the cold. Again."

"Shh." I put my hand against her chest again. "No more talking."

"Hey." She took my wrist and set my hand down on the bed. "I'm not gonna let you play me."

"I'm not playing you."

"Yeah, you are." She stood up. "I can't."

"What does that mean?"

"It means I like you. I want to go out with you. Like on dates."

I breathed out. "It doesn't work like that."

"You mean it doesn't work like that with me."

"I'm not going out with anyone else."

"You're not even going out with me."

I pushed my hands against the bed and got up. "Bobbie."

She looked away and shook her head. "I think you oughta go."

I ran out of the room and down the stairs so fast I almost bumped into Bobbie's sister. "Hi, Lauren. How's it going?"

She grinned at me. "You're really doing it?"

I inhaled. If tears stopped gathering between my eyelids right then, they would stay caught between my lashes like a film. My eyes would just look glossy, shiny, as long as nothing fell from them. "Doing what?"

"Debbing? This Friday?"

I nodded. "Yeah. You're coming, right?"

She followed me across the front hallway, her ponytail

bouncing behind her. "Who you going with?"

"My brother Al."

"Is it amazing?"

"It hasn't happened yet."

"No, I mean shopping for your dress, and dancing lessons, and rehearsals. Is it amazing?"

"Yeah. It's fun."

"Is your dress incredible?"

I nodded. "Yeah. I guess so. If you really like it you can borrow it in five years."

Lauren frowned and looked down at her twinset. "Six actually. Thanks though."

"Six then." I coughed to clear my throat. "I'll see you there."

I wiped the backs of my hands over my eyes, the robin's egg blue eye shadow Mom had gotten me smearing on the skin near my thumb.

Al looked up from his math book, flopped open on the dining room table. "Tragic final fitting?"

I looked away and tried to smile. "Yeah. Sure."

He cocked his head. "No really, what happened?"

I sniffed. "Yeah, right."

"Okay. You don't want to tell me. I get it." He tapped his pencil against the open book. "Is there anything I can get you? Tea? Vodka? Straight razor?"

I laughed. "Tea. Sure."

He snapped his fingers. "Aw, man. I thought I was about to become the sole inheritor."

He poured water from the kettle into the two mugs we had saved from just before Café Koko went under, the ones Al and I hid in the back of the cabinet so Mom wouldn't see they were chipped and throw them out during one of her clutter purges.

He handed me one, and I let the full, almost lemony scent rise in steam near my face.

"So is it"—he flipped over the empty tea bag package—" 'a wonderful way to relax and unwind any time of day?' "

I smiled. "I guess."

"So you gonna tell me now?"

I looked down at the kitchen floor. "I hurt a friend. Really badly."

He raised his eyebrows. "Friend?"

"Shut up."

"If you hurt somebody, why are you the one crying?"

I blew air out of my mouth until my body felt hollow. "I don't know. Because there's nothing I can do about it."

"There's always something you can do about it."

"Really."

"Really. Usually."

I nodded and held my palms against the sides of the cup. "Thanks for the tea."

"No problem." He raised his mug and clanked it against mine. "Cozy Chamomile and I aim to please."

My mother shook her head and trotted down the stairs, the sequins on her dress flashing in the light as her legs moved. "Poor thing."

I looked up from smoothing the tulle of my skirt. "What?"

"Your brother's sick."

"He's sick?"

"He can barely talk." She smoothed the edges of her lipstick in the hallway mirror.

I narrowed my eyes and looked up the stairs toward his room. "Let me see if he needs anything."

She turned around and looked at me. "That's really sweet

of you. Just make sure not to get anything on your dress, okay?
You look perfect. Like one of your dolls, remember them? Don't
mess yourself up."

I glided my hand along the banister. "I'm just going
upstairs."

I flicked on the light switch in Al's room.

"Oh, my stomach." Al groaned and peeked out from under
the covers with one eye. "Oh, it's you."

I sat on the edge of his bed and handed him a bottle of Orange
& Cream Jones'. "You're not sick."

"No. Not really. I just don't want to go to your stupid coming
out party with its disgusting rubber chicken."

"You're up to something."

He twisted off the cap and took a sip. "Yep."

"Afraid of being seen in a tux with your big sister?"

"Petrified."

"You could have just said you didn't want to do it. I would
have covered for you."

"I just now decided I couldn't face everyone wearing a bow
tie."

"Oh, yeah?" I fluffed my skirt over the bed. "Try doing it in
forty yards of tulle."

"I think I win with the bow tie."

"You do realize you're leaving me to come out into New
England society alone?"

"New England society?" He swallowed and sat up straight.
"Who're you kidding? New England society is Boston. Newport.
Not here. Look around. We're outnumbered by our cows."

I smiled. "You know, you shouldn't do this to Mom. She goes
white when you sneeze twice in a row."

"One day I'm gonna get a cold. I'm just preparing her."

I stood up and pulled my gloves up past my elbows. "You

better be on the sofa eating Ruffles when she gets back or she's gonna have a heart attack."

"But there won't be anything on."

I pulled the beanbag pillow from his desk chair and threw it at him. "See you later, coward."

"Takes one to know one."

I stopped in the doorway. "Excuse me?"

"You know what I'm talking about." He scooted the atom model a few inches toward the wall and set the soda bottle on the table next to his bed.

"I thought I'd find you here." My dad sat on the stone bench across from the swing set. "Is there a swing under there?"

I smiled and looked down. My skirt overflowed on either side of the swing, hiding the seat and burying a few inches of each chain in tulle.

"You know I'd be your escort." He straightened his lapels. "But I have to do the dad part. I've been training for the father-daughter waltz."

I laughed. "Glad to hear it."

"I know your brother's fine, by the way. You don't have to cover for him."

"Don't be mad at him." I kicked my satin pump in the gravel. "Would you really want to wear one of those things in front of a hundred girls if you were in the eighth grade?"

He chuckled. "Not on your life."

"Didn't think so."

"You look beautiful. Must be my good looks."

I grinned. "Why thank you."

"Any guy would be lucky." He stood up and brushed the dust from the granite bench off his hands. "I'll tell your mother you're getting some air."

I watched him cross the park back toward the hotel, the streetlights flickering as he got to the edge of the grass.

"What happened to your brother?"

I looked up, catching my breath in my chest when I saw her. "He's...not coming."

"Oh. Is he boycotting antiquated misogynist rituals?"

"It's not misogynist. It's fun."

Bobbie put her hands on the chains over my gloved fingers and pulled them back a little. "You're having fun?"

I dug my toes into the gravel, stopping the swing and looking up at her. "I want you."

She sighed. "I know."

"No." I laced my fingers between hers. "I want you. Tonight. I want you to be my escort."

She shook her head. "What?"

"You heard me."

"Do you have any idea how much trouble we'd get in? The Mob's got nothing on the League of Mother-Daughter Philanthropists."

"What would we get in trouble for? Like you said, it's legal in this state."

"Your mother would kill you."

"That would be *illegal*."

She laughed. "You're really serious about this."

"Yes." I stood up. "I am."

She looked at me. "You look beautiful, by the way."

"You clean up pretty good yourself." I flicked the bow tie, undone and draped over her neck. "This is easy. You just bow and then dance with me."

"I know it's easy. It's everything after this."

I shook my head. "I don't care." I put the tip of my finger to the corner of her mouth, a half-shade redder than usual, and smiled. "You wore the cherry kind?"

She shrugged. "Special occasion, special Chapstick."

"Evening, lovebirds." Al slid into the booth next to me.

I shoved his shoulder. "Oh, look who decided to show."

"I know." He heaved a sigh. "I just missed it."

"Mom tell you where I was?"

"Yeah." He looked at Bobbie. "And forgave me for aiding and abetting."

"Think she'll forgive me?" I asked.

"Pack your bags for an all-expense-paid guilt trip, but yeah, I think she will." He took a sip from my water glass. "Why aren't you two partying with the other cupcakes and penguins?"

"Yeah," I said. "Getting drunk on cheap beer and throwing up on my dress at Maureen Holson's after party. My idea of fun."

Bobbie nodded. "We thought we'd go for pie."

I pushed the plate toward Al. "It's cherry."

"And catch gay?" said Al. "No, thanks."

"You already like girls." Bobbie handed Al a fork. "It's too late."

THE ONLY GIRL I WANT

Sommer Marsden

C arla twisted her swizzle stick and frowned. "What do you mean? Like never?" She was huffy. And heavy. A huffy, heavy redhead with big green eyes and full pink lips. Her face, devoid of makeup, was peppered with freckles and as smooth as a baby's ass.

"Not for a while," I said with a shrug.

Maryann's reunion party was a nightmare. Half our college crowd was present, half of those married and toting screaming, runny-nosed toddlers. Another quarter were single, chic and trying to hide distasteful shudders as toddlers and babies wailed around us like some choir from hell. The other quarter was like me. Either not weighing in at all with their personal lives or proudly announcing that they had not only come out of the closet, but blown the closet door to kindling long ago. I had kissed Maryann's cheek upon arrival and said, "I'm gay."

"I know that." She had laughed then, her pale, friendly face lighting up with the laughter that uncoiled from her throat. I was mesmerized, as always. Completely and totally taken with her and the spattering of pale freckles that dotted her nose and her cheeks. Captivated by the café au lait hair that spilled from a plain silver clip. Crazy over her figure, fifteen pounds heavier than it had been and every pound stunning in the extra beauty it added.

"You do?"

"I've always known," she said and handed me a drink. "It's an Italian Surfer. Drink up."

"What do you mean you've always known?" I had swigged my Surfer like a fish.

"I mean, I have always known. I knew in high school." She waved a tray of shrimp puffs in my face. "Can I tempt you?"

I had taken a puff but didn't eat it. "Well, I sure as hell wish you would have told me. It would have made my high school years easier. And honey," I said, finding my bravado, "you've always tempted me."

Her lovely pale cheeks flooded with color and she dipped her head—her chin pointing to the floor, her eyes closing almost all the way, long sooty lashes touching the apples of her round cheeks. She looked like a Madonna in some Italian work of art: beautiful, kind, lush, and ripe. My body started to buzz with an overwhelming want to touch her. Maybe kiss her. A want accented with just enough regret, because I wouldn't get to. And I had been celibate long enough to know the drill, to switch off that part of myself like flipping a light switch. Celibate by choice. But Maryann was hard to resist. For me, she always had been.

Two hours had passed and I watched her play the crowd. Carla frowned at me. "Why would you do it, Stevie? Why would you be celibate on purpose when there is so much to sample? In this day and age, picking a sexual partner can be like making a grab bag of candy. A boy here, a girl there, a boy and a girl after a dinner of pasta. Maybe an orgy. A threesome, a foursome, a moresome."

I kept waiting for her to laugh or even smile to show that she was joking, but she didn't. She just went on glaring at me with that big green gaze, looking half flabbergasted, half angry. Like I had somehow betrayed women everywhere by not getting laid every four seconds.

"Maybe that's why I did it," I said with a shrug. "Plus, I don't switch off with the whole guy today, girl tomorrow thing. Not my deal. I like women. Period. End of story. And I just want one person, I don't need a menagerie."

She blinked again and I wondered for just a second if she was going to punch me. Monogamy! What was I thinking? Why have one special person when you can have one special person a day? I almost laughed but thought better of it. Instead, I finished my Italian Surfer and excused myself.

"Where are you going?" she demanded. Though we hadn't been friends in college, she acted as if we had and had latched on to me the moment I entered.

"I think I'll go mingle, grab a plate, another drink," I muttered. I backed away slowly. The same way I had read you should back away from a bear should you happen upon one. "I'll be back. Don't worry."

I was totally lying.

"Stevie! Stevie!" I glanced around to see George waving wildly. Even in our freshman year of college, his name had been Boy George. George was one of the first young gay men I had met who was totally open about who he was. His sexuality was not a secret. At all. He had been one of my heroes. One of the first to urge me to tell my parents the truth and claim my own identity.

"Hey, there!" I went to him and he gathered me in his generous arms. He'd somehow gone from a rail-thin boy in pegged jeans and false eyelashes to a tall, plushy man with gorgeous skin and a double chin. "Oh, my god, you look fab."

"You mean fat," he quipped.

"No, you look gorgeous, love. Really." A slight younger man stood behind him, grinning with a mix of love and pride.

"And you, darling Stevie, look sex starved."

"What?" I was shocked and then not. Leave it to George to zero right in on the sex—or lack thereof. "How can you possibly...? Never mind."

"Your eyes are not as shiny, your hair is a little lank, and you look a tad pinched. Don't get me wrong, Stevie, you look incredible, but get laid and you will be a showstopper."

Only George could evoke instant honesty, so as he fixed my arm in the crook of his, I whispered, "I'm voluntarily celibate, thank you very much."

"Oh, heavens me!" he said in a big garish voice. Everything about George was big and loud and bright. He was a walking work of art in his paint-splashed, tent-sized shirt and hot pink bowling shoes. "Say it ain't so." Then he winked quickly. "Speaking of hot monkey sex, this is my boy toy of the day, Todd."

The thin love-struck man stepped forward and shook my hand. His voice was so soft I had to strain to hear him. "Nice to meet you, Stevie. I've heard stories."

"Of the day, eh?" I wasn't buying it.

Todd blushed and laughed. "For the last six years."

"That's a long day," I joked, elbowing George.

"It's just a fling!" he said, waving me off. I noticed that they wore matching silver bands on the ring fingers of their left hands. I didn't push it, though. George had always been phobic about commitment. I was just glad to see him happy. "It'll be over before you know it."

Todd smiled at me and I smiled back. "Mmm-hmm."

At the bar, we ordered drinks. I caught sight of Maryann, kissing cheeks, shaking hands, serving shrimp puffs. She looked across the room at me and grinned. My heart seized up a bit. I wanted her to kiss my cheek. Wanted her to sit and talk to me into the wee hours while we got drunk and gossiped. All that good stuff—I wanted it. But I wanted more. So much more. She was the only girl I wanted, and for a long time, too. So I'd stopped with other women. Just until I could get my head on straight, or meet someone who could make me forget the person I wanted the most. Who was also the one girl I could not have. Ever.

I swallowed around the newly bloomed lump in my throat and realized that George was following my gaze and I was now under his eagle-eyed scrutiny. "So, celibacy, you say. Is that possibly due to some unrequited love? Some longing? Some Romeo and Juliet dealio? Or let's say Rita and Juliet, shall we."

I laughed but the lump in my throat seemed to grow instead of shrink. I accepted my Italian Surfer from the bartender and dropped a dollar in the tip cup. "No way. She's just a friend."

"Because she has to be. And I am just a shy and quiet queen," he bellowed and tossed his imaginary boa over his shoulder. Todd hid a smile with his hands but his shoulders shook with laughter.

"Yes, George. You are a wallflower if I've ever seen one. "

"Yes, yes. I know. I really need to loosen up a bit. Now what are you drinking?"

"An Italian Surfer," I said. They really were addictive. Not like my normal red wine or beer. Sweet without being cloying, they were sliding down easily. Maybe a bit too easily.

"Ah." George took my arm and led me out to the patio. "I had an Italian surfer once. Such a flexible young man. His name was Paolo."

Todd cleared his throat and sipped his Corona.

"Sorry, love, sorry. How rude of me." George leaned in and said, "He's so possessive even though this is just a fling."

I laughed out loud and sipped more of my drink. "You're a heartbreaker, George."

"What can I say?" he shrugged and to my horror, when Maryann shot past, he snagged her slender arm and gripped her in a bear hug that shook his colorful shirt and made Todd shake his head. "Sweet young Maryann! Thank you so much for putting this shindig together. You are a gem! A gem. And this is Todd. Todd is my boy toy. And you know Stevie. Of course you do. How many nights did you two get drunk and talk? And you shared a dorm room. And classes. And probably panties!"

He was booming and I was trying to back away from him. His voice was megaphone worthy and heads were turning left and right. Most knew Georgie and they just shook their heads and returned to the party. Some spouses and partners looked confused but amused. Maryann looked both and she also looked to me and mouthed the words, *Help me.*

"Maybe you need to cut back on the drinks," Todd said gently.

All of us knew Georgie was fine. Well, all of us but Maryann and now I saw exactly what my friend was doing. He was like the diversion during a con. The flash and bang that drew attention while pockets were picked and purses were lifted. Now Maryann was giving me a desperate look of appeal, for me to save her. From George. Which was just too fucking funny but I was not one to look a gift George in the mouth and I wanted to know what all the blushing and head-ducking from earlier had been about.

"Let's go make some coffee." I gently tugged Maryann from his corpulent grip and pulled her to me just enough to feel the flare of her hip against my waist. My nipples peaked and my body went somehow tight and soft all at once. God, I wanted to kiss her. Instead, I said, "You'd like some coffee, wouldn't you George?"

"I'd love some coffee. And when you come back, let's discuss those panties."

Maryann cringed just a bit, but as we turned, Georgie dropped me a wink and I stifled a laugh—clever, lovely bastard. I was mortified and excited all at once. I guided Maryann by her slender shoulders to her kitchen. We pushed through the swinging doors and the sudden silence was deafening.

"Oh, my god! Thank you. I see Boy George is shy as ever." She laughed, making a pot of coffee with barely a glance. She backed up and bumped me, for just an instant. Just long enough for me to feel the soft swell of her ass against my pelvis, her shoulder blades banging my breasts. Just long enough to get a face full of her long shiny hair and for the lemongrass scent of it to fill my head. "Oops," she said, and I steadied her with my hands on her waist.

I closed my eyes to balance my mind. The cotton crotch of my panties had gone wet, my mind fuzzy. I took a step back and tried to busy myself. I found a photo of Maryann with another dark-haired girl. I assumed they were at Disney World, what with the Mickey Mouse ears and Goofy standing in the middle. "Who's this?" I asked, trying to distract myself. There was a mild resemblance. Probably a cousin or something.

"My ex." She frowned, took the photo from me and shoved it in a drawer. "I thought I had taken it down." She caught my look and frowned again. "What?" Before I could answer she was rummaging for mugs and a tray. I watched her lean back in her white sleeveless blouse, stared at her perfect ass in her black capris, her perfect feet tucked into white flats that were painted with irises. The shoes resembled porcelain, something a princess would wear. I realized my ears were buzzing and I felt light-headed. I must have looked it, because when Maryann turned she came to me. "Stevie? Are you okay? Sit down."

I let her push me onto a stool in the corner and push a wet paper towel to my forehead. "I'm fine." I was lying.

Maryann leaned in. "You don't look okay. You look sick. And a bit pissed. What is—"

I cut her off when I kissed her. I dropped the paper towel and pushed my hands into her hair and yanked her forward so she lost her balance. She fell against me, struggling for a moment and then her hands settled on my shoulders and she leaned into the kiss. Kissing me back. Kissing me soft and then hard and it was all so easy, just as I had imagined.

"You said you knew I was gay," I said.

She nodded, tracing my bottom lip with the tip of her finger. "Yeah."

"Because you were gay?" I kissed her again, biting her bottom lip till she squealed. I wanted to inflict a little pain, so very, very pissed and relieved was I.

"I was pretty sure." She pushed her hands into my short black hair and yanked so that I cringed. She pulled me forward by my hair and kissed me again. Then she turned and slid a bolt on the kitchen door, effectively locking us in and keeping the door from swinging.

"And you neglected to tell me that particular part." I bit her lip again and she squirmed, pushing between the V of my legs so that she stood rooted between my thighs. Her fingers tickled over the zipper of my jeans and a steady pulse started in my pussy. My hips shot up to meet her hand and she tsked.

"You should behave." She popped the button and worked the zipper.

"I am so fucking pissed. And horny. Why? Why didn't you tell me?" I pushed my hand down the front of her capris, past a silky pair of panties, and shoved my fingers into her cunt. She was wet. Very wet. Wet for me. Fucking finally, wet for me after all these years. I hooked my fingers as her eyes rolled back a bit, and I tugged her forward with my fingers. She leaned in and kissed me some more.

"I'm sorry. By the time I knew, you were with someone. Then I was. I never wanted to step on toes. I never wanted to hurt anyone." She pushed at my waistband and dropped to her knees, her hot breath on the front of my white cotton panties. I was suddenly boneless and brainless and I stared, waiting for, *willing* her lips on me. On my clit, on my body. Sucking me, making me come. Making me say her name over and over again. I stared. Then she said, "I hear you're celibate."

My hips tipped up again, a completely involuntary response, trying so hard to meet those plump gorgeous lips. How many times had I fantasized about that mouth on me? "Not for you," I said.

"Why celibate?" she asked, trailing a fingertip over the seam of my pussy. I could feel the plain simple white cotton soaking up my juices. A flutter worked deep inside of me and I wondered if I would come before anything happened at all.

"I was having way too much meaningless sex and couldn't seem to find the right girl."

She frowned again. "That's sad. Is there a right girl for you?"

"You are the right girl for me," I blurted. "I've known that since college."

"So you gave up girls? Because I was taken? Surely there was another girl." She put her mouth over my pussy, her breath snaking through the cotton, soaking me in warmth. Her lips on me but not. Her mouth on me but not. Her tongue a heartbeat from my clit.

I wanted to bang my head against the wall, or shove aside my panties and pull her to me. Instead I said, "You're the only girl I want. So I gave them up. Until I could...figure it out."

Her big dark eyes looked up from between my thighs and she tugged my panties down. I lifted my foot from the stool bar and she tossed them in the corner before spreading my thighs. Her lips were even softer than I imagined. Her tongue a demon, making me ready to swear anything, everything she wanted. Her long slim fingers worked into me as I bucked up on the stool seat to meet her mouth, to drive her fingers deeper. The first orgasm gripped me and I threw my head back. I bit my lip and tasted blood as my whole body shook with it. Better and faster and more perfect than I had ever thought an orgasm could be. Her hair was soft under my fingers. "God, Mar, that was—"

Her tongue was back, her mouth sucking at me. Her lips playing over my supersensitive pussy until I danced on the seat a bit, too sensitive but too good to push her away. She ate me slower this time, pushing four long fingers into me, and I parted easily. She fucked me in slower thrusts of her digits, fluttered her fingers, stroked my G-spot. Played me perfectly, as if we'd been together a thousand times before. I was crying just a little at finally being where we were. After all the time and the fantasies, I wanted to pinch myself to make sure it was real. But then Maryann bit the inside of my thigh and I let out a bark of pleasure and pain and came around her hand, harder than the first time, longer than the first time. My body went soft and warm.

"You taste exactly like I thought," she said. Her lips moved over my skin and she left wet trails of my moisture as she went. Her mouth found mine and I kissed her hard, pulling her to me a bit too hard because part of me feared she'd walk away.

"What? What do I taste like?"

Maryann kissed over my face, down my throat. She pinched my nipples and someone knocked on the door. "You taste right. You taste like raspberries and honey and cinnamon. Clean cotton and wood smoke and ocean air. All of my favorite things."

I touched her hair and slid my hand back along her pussy, pushing a finger inside of her to test her. When the strength returned to my legs I was going to fuck her senseless. Then more banging on the door.

Maryann grinned. "We'd better open that door before someone breaks it down."

"But I want to...this wasn't..." I sighed. "God. That wasn't pity sex was it?"

She stopped and I thought she was pissed. Then her shoulders were shaking with laughter and she grabbed my face, her lips everywhere at once. "You are so dense. I had this reunion party to get you here. I plotted and planned like a shameless hussy."

Relief flooded through me. When more pounding came, I yelled, "Hold on for god's sake!"

"Let's go. We'll give Georgie his coffee and I'll give you a tour."

I took the coffee tray from her. She slid the bolt back but didn't release the door. I didn't really want a tour. God, I finally had her, had a chance at her, *with* her, and she wanted to give me a tour?

She read my mind like she had in college when I was stressing and obsessing. "We'll start the tour in my bedroom, 'kay?"

I let out a grateful sigh and followed her out to Georgie.

"Coffee," I said, setting the tray down.

"Ah, there you go." He laughed, eyeing me and no doubt noting the sex glow on my face, the grin I couldn't hide. He turned to Todd. "See, I told you. Get her laid and she'd be a showstopper."

I would have been a bit embarrassed but Maryann had me by the arm and I had other things to think about.

FIVE

Cheyenne Blue

When Mary leaves Tess after five years together, a hole forms in Tess's heart and expands until her whole chest is one gaping ache of emptiness. Each press of Mary's lips to the nape of Tess's neck has drawn out a small piece of her soul, wisp by wisp, as insubstantial as smoke, sucked away by Mary's lips. And so when Mary leaves the Denver apartment for the final time with a careless wave of her hand, a kiss that fails to connect, and an airy, "See ya around, babe," Tess is left not just alone, but empty.

Insubstantial, as if the best pieces of her life have drifted out of the door with Mary. Tess's favorite CDs certainly have, along with the TV, so she's left in an echoing apartment with only a wailing Joni Mitchell for company. Tess rocks on the couch, staring at the darker square on the wall where her Salvador Dali print used to hang and presses her fist against her breastbone, as if she could reach in and take hold of that frightening emptiness and throw it out the window into the frigid Denver winter. But the window is sealed shut and the stone in her chest won't go so easily.

The day that Mary leaves, Tess closes the door on the apartment they had shared and walks down to Washington Park. The lake is partially frozen and small ice floes creak on the frigid brown water. Tess walks down the tiny stretch of sand by the boathouse and only stops when the slush covers the toes of her boots. She stares down at the oily water seeping into the fine leather. *That will stain*, she thinks objectively. *These boots will be ruined.*

Deliberately, she walks a pace farther into the lake, crunching through the ice so that the water curls over her ankles. Ruined boots, ruined life. She tests the concept on her tongue, waits to embrace the pain, waits to feel the knot of misery that weights her chest expand farther, but this time it's swamped by irritation that she's wrecked her boots. The cold numbs her feet, and she turns and stomps back to dry land.

Tess becomes a walking cliché for love lost. Her face takes on a haunted look, hollow cheeked from the churning in her stomach that refuses to let her eat more than a few bites. Her hair hangs lank, dull and stringy, and her eyes are welded straight ahead. For why look around at the world when your world has gone?

The pads of flesh melt off her hips and belly, leaving her with the willowy boyish figure she's always yearned for, but she takes no pleasure in it. Without Mary to run fingers over her newly concave stomach, to drum patterns on her jutting hip bone, what's the point?

The winter rolls on, and Tess changes jobs. Her new office is on South Broadway and now, instead of taking the bus, she leaves the apartment each morning and drifts down the streets, engulfed in a river of people who all seem more purposeful than she. Five blocks to Colfax, then five blocks to Broadway and then five blocks south to the corner of Tenth Avenue. Five weeks since Mary left. Five days in the working week, leaving two days for mourning and crying.

Each day, she wakes in the morning and listens to the first thought that comes to her: *Mary is gone, I am alone.* The bed is empty and there's little chance of filling it as long as she keeps avoiding the small Denver scene, too afraid of bumping into Mary flaunting a new love on her arm. Her nights are filled with rental DVDs, Star Trek reruns and long rambling monologues when she berates the bottle of Wild Turkey for letting Mary leave her.

She buys a pair of flannel pajamas and wears them in bed, letting the soft material comfort and embrace her. On weekends, she seldom leaves the house, except on Sunday mornings when she buys the papers and walks through Cheesman Park to the bagel place where the gay boys hang out. It's a safe bet that she won't see Mary there, and the company of queer folk is reassuring.

There's a girl behind the counter, a wiry, skinny sort of kid with a pixie face. In an earlier lifetime, Tess would have found her interesting, attractive even. She has clear gray eyes and a cap of shiny nutmeg hair. Her movements are fast and contained, with no excess of gesture. She always smiles at Tess on those Sunday mornings, as Tess orders her cranberry bagel and latte, and Tess smiles back in an abstracted way, her mind already turning to the headlines and grocery coupons of the Sunday paper.

After a few Sundays, Tess finds she's looking out for her, and instead of waiting for her coffee with her eyes fixed on the menu board above the counter, her eyes follow Pixie-Face as she stretches for the coffee flavorings, bends for the milk, reaches into the glass cabinet for a muffin.

One week, Pixie-Face is absent, and instead there's a man behind the counter. Tess takes her coffee outside that day, sits on the patio in the March sunshine.

But the next week Pixie-Face is back. "You weren't here last week," Tess blurts out, and then blushes, aware that she sounds accusatory, stalkerish.

The girl smiles. "Vacation. I was mountain biking in Moab. Me and a friend went down and camped."

"Oh." A vague precursor of disappointment seeps into Tess's blood. "I hope you had a good time."

The girl gives her a slight smile. "I did, yeah. But Marlie—my friend—broke her collarbone. Here's your coffee." And she turns away to serve the next customer.

Tess puts a dollar in the tip jar and takes her coffee to one of the slouchy couches that ring the room, and tells herself that her decision to sit where she can see the counter is because otherwise the light would be in her eyes.

The next week, as she's walking to work, she sees Mary leaving a diner on Colfax, laptop beneath one arm, the other around the shoulders of a girl. Tess sees them kiss in the doorway, sees the way their mouths move together. She squeezes her eyes tightly shut against the pain and keeps walking, and when she jolts down off the curb and her eyes open, she sees Mary looking straight at her, a slight frown of irritation creasing her brow.

"Hi Tess," Mary says evenly, her arm holding the other girl tightly to her.

"Hi." Tess keeps walking, but her eyes remain open this time, and she concentrates on her feet, marching in even beat along the sidewalk.

Five paces to the corner, five blocks to work, five days to her birthday, five weeks to her vacation—not that she has decided where to go.

That evening, she contemplates her couch and the DVDs she's rented for the week, and then she sees how the evening light falls across the polished floorboards, and hears the trill of an early spring bird. Throwing aside her slouchy pajamas, she reaches for a pair of gym shoes and some jogging pants. They hang on her hips from all the weight she's lost.

Outside the door, she turns her face up to the sky and heads for the park. It's a mild evening, and the park is full of couples strolling and joggers circling. There's a boisterous touch football game happening at one end, and Tess stops to watch. A scruffy dog appears and joins the game, tripping the players and eventually making off with the ball, to the players' dismay. Tess smiles into the setting sun, watching the dog evade attempts at capture. Eventually, a compact woman in red shorts is able to grab him as he goes by, and the ball is recaptured. With a start of surprise, Tess recognizes the girl from the bagel cafe.

She finds a tree to rest her back against and watches as the game resumes. Pixie-Face's team loses, although she manages a touchdown. As the game winds down, Tess sets her feet for home and treats herself to Pad Thai and a glass of wine from the new noodle place for dinner.

"I saw you last week," says Pixie-Face, when Tess orders her cranberry bagel. "Watching the game."

"Hmm," says Tess, noncommittal, even though there's a warmth in her chest knowing that Pixie-Face noticed her among the hurly-burly of an energetic game.

"I looked for you when we'd finished, but you were gone. I was wondering if—"

"Hey, Morag! Snappy with that two percent. Customers are waiting!"

Morag's boss's yell cuts off whatever she was going to say, and

Tess resists the urge to reach out and grab her by the shoulder and demand she finish the sentence.

"Later," says Morag, and with a flick of nutmeg hair, she's gone, scooping up the carton of 2 percent and a cloth for wiping tables.

Tess takes her coffee to the slouchy couches and pretends to read the *Westword*. Even though she hangs around for longer this Sunday, Morag is busy and doesn't return. She walks home through the park, watching the dogs chase squirrels, and enjoys the sun gleaming on the snowcaps in the distance, way, way over the city.

Slowly, the real world grasps her again and she starts going out with the girls from work. She joins a book club, takes a class in kite making and goes with her classmates down to Cherry Creek Reservoir where they hoist their gaudy creations aloft so they dance on the breeze like sailboats on the ocean. She still goes to the bagel cafe on Sundays, and if Thursday evenings often find her wandering the park in search of a touch football game, well, what of it?

Five months, she thinks one day. It's been five months since Mary left. Five times five pounds of fat she's lost. Five weeks since her vacation in Hawaii, and five years, five months, and five days since her first date with Mary. She sits carefully on the couch to analyze that. Head: still okay, still sane. Body: still working. Heart: still beating, maybe a little bit hollow from being alone but still in one piece.

She's determined the next Sunday. She's going to trap Morag against the pastry counter, ask her for a date. Maybe she likes Thai food. Maybe she likes Sushi. Dinner, a nice restaurant. Wine.

She goes earlier than usual, hoping it will be quiet. As she approaches, she can see Morag's cap of hair behind the counter, sees her chatting to a customer, who turns and saunters out, holding a takeout coffee.

It's Mary, and she's alone.

For a moment, Tess thinks of ducking into an alley, turning around and going back the way she came, but that's pointless, as Mary's seen her, and she's slowing to a stop, a smile—a genuine Mary smile—on her face.

"Hey, babe. Been too long! How ya been?"

"I'm fine. Busy." She studies Mary, who is studying her appreciatively. A frisson of pride surges through her at the appreciation in Mary's eyes.

"You look great! Lost a ton of weight. You started running or something?"

Tess shrugs. "Walking, healthy eating. A good vacation."

There are dark smudges under Mary's eyes, and Tess sees the extra chubbiness in her face.

"You got time for a coffee? There's a place just here where I get takeout. Very cute waitress."

"Not really," Tess hedges. "I need to be getting along."

"Okay." Mary hesitates. "You seeing anyone? I'm between dates at the moment, so if you wanted to meet up sometime, for old time's sake...?"

A spurt of irritation. Mary wants a quick fuck until someone better comes along?

"I don't think that's a good idea."

"Pity. We were always good together, and you look very hot now you've dropped those excess pounds."

Tess doesn't answer, holds herself still on the sidewalk, resisting the urge to shuffle her feet, waiting to see what Mary will do. The pause stretches uncomfortably.

"Well, see ya around sometime." Mary nods and strides off, flipping the top of her coffee to take a mouthful.

Tess waits until she's turned the corner then paces the remaining few steps into the bagel place. It's still early, and Morag is putting the muffins onto trays.

"Hi," she says when she sees Tess. "Cranberry bagel and a latte?"

"Actually," says Tess, "I have to ask you something before I lose my nerve."

She didn't plan that. The words were out of her mouth before she thought. But once they're out, hanging in the coffee-scented air, she knows it's the right time.

"Oh?" Morag cocks a hip on the side of the counter and waits.

"I was wondering if you'd like to come out for dinner one night. Sushi, Thai, whatever you like best."

Morag chokes a laugh and Tess dies a little inside.

"Sorry," says Morag. "I'm not laughing at you. I'm chuckling at the timing. It's been months since anyone noticed me in that way, and now in ten minutes I've been asked out twice. Did you see the woman with the bleached hair who left just before you came in? She asked me out as well."

Mary. Tess wilts. How can she compete?

"Did you accept?" she asks.

Morag smiles. "No. I was tempted, but I put her off. And now I'm glad I did." Tess dares to hope, just a little.

"Thai is my favorite. I'd love to go with you."

Relief courses through her veins. "In that case, I'll have a toasted cranberry bagel with cream cheese and a latte."

Morag's eyes crinkle. "What would you have had if I'd said no?"

"I'd have left," confesses Tess, "and consoled my broken heart with eggs Benedict at Pete's Diner on Colfax."

"Bagels are better for you."

"Thai it is then. How about Friday night?"

"Friday is fine." Morag gestures to the end of the counter. "I'll bring your coffee out."

The end of the counter is hidden from casual eyes in the cafe or the street. Morag places the latte down and her hand reaches for Tess's, lacing their fingers together. With a tug, she pulls Tess a pace toward her. Soft lips brush Tess's cheek for a second, whispering over her lips in a breath of espresso.

"I'm looking forward to it." And Morag is gone, back behind the muffin counter to serve the boys who have just walked in.

Tess takes her coffee to the couch and sits so that her eyes can follow Morag.

Five hours until the bagel shop closes, five sections of the Sunday paper to read. Five days in the working week and five days until her date with Morag.

Five days until her new life.

THE OUTSIDE EDGE

Sacchi Green

Suli was fire and wine, gold and scarlet, lighting up the dim passageway where we waited.

I leaned closer to adjust her Spanish tortoiseshell comb. A cascade of dark curls brushed my face, shooting sparks all the way down to my toes, but even a swift, tender kiss on her neck would be too risky. I might not be able to resist pressing hard enough to leave a dramatic visual effect the TV cameras couldn't miss.

Tenderness wasn't what she needed right now, and neither was passion. An edgy outlet for nervous energy would be more like it. "Skate a clean program," I murmured in her ear, "and maybe I'll let you get dirty tonight." My arm across her shoulders might have looked locker-room casual, but the look she shot me had nothing to do with team spirit.

"*Maybe*, Jude? You think maybe you'll *let* me?" She tossed her head. Smoldering eyes, made even brighter and larger by theatrical makeup, told me that I'd need to eat my words later before my mouth could move on to anything more appealing.

The other pairs were already warming up. Suli followed Tim into the arena, her short scarlet skirt flipping up oh-so-accidentally to reveal her firm, sweet ass. She wriggled, daring me to give it an encouraging slap, knowing all too well what the rear view of a scantily clad girl does for me.

I followed into the stadium and watched the action from just outside the barrier. As Suli and Tim moved onto the ice, the general uproar intensified. Their groupies had staked a claim near one end, and a small cadre of my own fans were camped out nearby, having figured out over the competition season that something was up between us. Either they'd done some discreet stalking, or relied on the same gaydar that had told them so much about me even before I'd fully understood it myself. Probably both.

Being gay wasn't, in itself, a career-buster these days. Sure, the rumormongers were eternally speculating about the men in their sequined outfits, but the skating community was united in a compact never to tell, and the media agreed tacitly never to ask. A rumor of girl-on-girl sex would probably do nothing more than inspire some fan fiction in certain blogging communities. That didn't mean there weren't still lines you couldn't cross in public, especially in performance—lines I was determined, with increasing urgency, to cross once and for all.

But I didn't want to bring Suli down if I fell. That discussion was something we kept avoiding, and whenever I tried to edge toward it she'd distract me in ways I couldn't resist.

Suli's the best, I thought now in the stadium, watching her practice faultless jumps with Tim. You'd never guess what she'd been doing last night with me, while the other skaters were preparing for the performance of their lives with more restful rituals. She'd already set records in pairs skating, and next year, at my urging, she was going to go solo. It was a good thing I wouldn't be competing against her.

I won't be competing against anybody, I thought, my mind wandering as the warm-up period dragged on.

It had taken me long enough to work it out, focusing on my skating for so many years, but the more I appreciated the female curves inside those scanty, seductive costumes, the less comfortable I was wearing them. Cute girls in skimpy outfits were just fine with me—bodies arched in laybacks, or racing backward, glutes tensed and pumping, filmy fabric fluttering in the breeze like flower petals waving to the hungry bees—but I'd rather see than be one.

I'd have quit mainstream competition if they hadn't changed the rules to allow long-legged "unitards" instead of dresses. That concession wasn't enough to make me feel really comfortable, though, and I knew my coach was right that some judges would hold it against me if I didn't wear a skirt at least once in a while. This year I'd alternated animal-striped unitards with a Scottish outfit just long enough to preserve the mystery of what a Scotsman wears under his kilt, assuming that he isn't doing much in the way of spins or jumps or spirals. I knew this for certain, having experimented in solitary practice with my own sturdy six inches of silicon pride.

So why not just switch to the Gay Games? Or follow Rudy Galindo and Surya Bonaly to guest appearances on SkateOut's Cabaret on Ice?

If you have a shot at the Olympics, the Olympics are where you go, that's why. Or so I'd thought. But I was only in fifth place after the short program—maybe one or two of the judges weren't that keen on bagpipe music—and a medal was too long a shot now.

I knew, deep down, what the problem was. Johanna, the

coach we shared, had urged me to study Suli's style in hopes that some notion of elegance and grace might sink into my thick head. Suli had generously agreed to try to give me at least a trace of an artistic clue. But the closer we became, the more I'd rebelled against faking a feminine grace and elegance that were so naturally hers, and so unnatural for me.

This would be my last competition, no matter what. Maybe I'd get a pro gig with a major ice show, maybe I wouldn't. If I did, it would be on my own terms. "As God is my witness, I'll never be girlie again!" I'd proclaimed melodramatically to Suli last night.

"Works just fine for me," she'd said, kneeling with serene poise to take my experimental six inches between her glossy, carmined lips and deep into her velvet throat.

Ten minutes later, serenity long gone, I stood braced against the edge of the bed and bore her weight while she clamped her thighs around my hips and her cunt around my pride, locked her hands behind my neck, and rode me with fierce, pounding joy. I dug my fingers into her asscheeks to steady her, and to add to the driving force of her lunges. Small naked breasts slapped against mine on each forward stroke. When I could catch one succulent nipple in my mouth her cries would rise to a shriller pitch, but then she'd jerk roughly away to get more leverage for each thrust.

My body ached with strain and arousal and the friction of the harness. My mind was a blur of fantasies. *We're whirling in the arena, my skates carving spirals into the ice, her dark hair lifting in the wind...*

"Spin me!" Suli suddenly arched her upper body into a layback position, arms no longer gripping me but raised into a pleading curve. Adrenaline, muscles, willpower; none of it was enough now. Only speed could keep us balanced. I stepped back from the bed and spun in place, swinging her in one wide circle, then another, tension hammering through my clit hard enough to counter the burn of the leather gouging my flesh.

Suli's voice whipped around us, streaming as free as her hair. I held on, battling gravity, riding the waves of her cries, until, as they crested, the grip of her legs around me began to slip. In two lurching steps I had her above the bed again, and in another second she was on the sheets. I pressed on until her breathing began to slow, then covered her tender breasts and mouth with a storm of kisses close to bites until I had to arch back and pump and grind my way to a noisy release of my own.

When we'd sprawled together in delirious exhaustion long enough for our panting to ease, I raised up to gaze at her. The world-famous princess of poise and grace lay tangled in her own wild hair, lips swollen, skin streaked with sweat, and most likely bruised in places where the TV cameras had better not reach.

"And *you* lectured *me* about never jumping without knowing exactly where I was going to land!" I said. "How did you know I wouldn't drop you?"

"Aren't you always bugging me to let you try lifts?" she countered drowsily. "You've spun me before, on the ice; you're tall and strong enough." She rolled over on top of me and murmured into the hollow of my throat, "Anyway, I did know where I was going to land. And I knew that you'd get me there. You always do." Then her head slumped onto my shoulder and her body slid down to nestle in the protective curve of mine. In seconds she was asleep.

I always will, I mouthed silently, but couldn't say it aloud. Giving way to tenderness, to emotions deeper than the pyrotechnics of sex, was more risk than I could handle. Wherever I was going to land, she belonged somewhere better. *How am I going to bear it? How can we still be together?*

* * *

I shook my head to clear it. Suli and Tim were gliding with the rest of the competitors toward the edge of the ice, and I realized suddenly that it was time to take my seat in the stands. The final grouping of the pairs long program was about to get underway.

Suli and Tim skated third, to music from Bizet's *Carmen*. Somebody always skates to *Carmen*, but no one ever played the part better than Suli. The dramatic theme of love and betrayal was a perfect setting for her, and today the passionate beat of the "Habanera" was a perfect match for my jealous mood.

Watching Tim with Suli on the ice always drove me crazy. When his hand slid from the small of her back to her hip I wanted to lunge and chew it off at the wrist. His boyfriend Thor, a speed skater with massively muscled thighs, would have been highly displeased by that, so it was just as well that I resisted the impulse.

It wasn't really the way Tim touched Suli that burned me. Well, okay, maybe it was, with every nuance of the traditional lifts and holds pulsing with erotic innuendo. Still, my hands knew her needs far better than he ever could, or cared to. But he was allowed to do it publicly, artistically, acting out scenarios of fiery love—and I wasn't. Knowing that the delectable asscheeks filling the taut scarlet seat of her costume bore bruises in the shapes of my fingers was only small comfort.

His other hand rested lightly on her waist as they whirled across the ice. Any second—in six more beats—she would jump, and with simultaneous precision he would lift, and throw... *Now!* For all the times I'd seen it, my breath still caught. Suli twisted impossibly high into the air, and far out...out...across the ice...

Yes! Throw triple axel! A perfect one-footed landing flowing into a smooth, graceful follow-through, then up into a double loop side by side with Tim in clockwork synchronicity.

It was the best. The audience knew it, the judges knew it. I knew it, and admiration nearly won out over envy when Tim lifted Suli high overhead, her legs spread wide, in the ultimate hand-in-crotch position known as the Helicopter. Envy surged back. Her crotch would be damp with sweat and excitement, not the kind I could draw from her, but still! Then she dropped abruptly past his face, thighs briefly scissoring his neck, pussy nudging his chin. I shook, nearly whimpering, as Suli slid sensuously down along Tim's body. As soon as her blades touched down she leaned back, back, impossibly far back, until her hair brushed the ice in a death spiral. I tensed as though my hand, not Tim's, gripped hers to brace her just this side of disaster.

A few judges always took points off for "suggestive" material. What did they think pairs skating was all about, if not sex? But it was a technically clean and ambitious program, beautifully executed. Suli and Tim won the gold medals they deserved.

I got no chance to go for the gold of Suli's warm body that night. When I came up behind her in our room and reached around to cup her breasts, she wriggled her compact butt against me, then turned and shoved me away.

"No," she decreed, putting a finger across my lips as I tried to speak. I nibbled at it instead. "You have your long program tomorrow, and I know better than you do what you need."

I tried to object, with no luck.

"Sure," Suli went on, "fast and furious sex and complete exhaustion were just what I needed, but you'll do better saving up that energy and channeling the tension into your skating."

"It doesn't matter," I said sulkily. "I can't medal now anyway. I was thinking, in fact, that this might as well be the time..."

She knew what I meant. "No!" Her scowl was at least as

alluring as her smiles. "You can still win the bronze, if you want it enough. At least two of those prima donnas ahead of you have never skated a clean long program in their lives. Medal, and you get into the exhibition at the end. That's the time to make your grand statement to the world." She saw my hesitation, and gripped my shoulders so hard her nails dug in. "Think of Johanna! You can't disgrace your coach during actual competition. And think of your fans!" Her expression eased into a smile she couldn't suppress. Her grip eased. "Okay, your fans would love every minute of it. I've seen the signs they flip at you when they're sure the cameras can't see. WE WANT JUDE, PREFERABLY IN THE NUDE!" She drew her fingers lightly across my chest and downward. "Can't say that I blame them."

Suli was so close that her warm scent tantalized me. I thought I was going to get some after all, but the kiss I grabbed was broken off all too soon, leaving me aching for more.

"Please Jude, do it this way." She stroked my face, brushing back my short dark hair. I wasn't sure I could bear her gentleness. "Even your planned routine comes close enough to the edge. One way or another, it will be worth it. I promise."

So I did it her way, and skated the long program I'd rehearsed so many times. Inside, though, I was doing it my way at last, and not much caring if it showed.

I skated to a medley from the Broadway show *Cats*. My black unitard with white down the front and at the cuffs was supposed to suggest a "tuxedo" cat with white paws. The music swept from mood to mood, poignance to nostalgia to swagger, but no matter what character a song was meant to suggest, in my mind and gut I was never, for a moment, anybody's sweet pussy. I was every inch a Tom. Tomcat prowling urban roofs and alleys; tomboy tumbling the dairymaid in the hay; top-hatted Tom in the back streets of Victorian London pinching the housemaids' cheeks, fore and aft.

Suli had been right about storing up tension and then letting it spill out. Like fantasy during sex, imagination sharpened my performance. Each move was linked to its own notes of the music, practiced often enough to be automatic, but tonight my footwork was more precise, my spins faster, my jumps higher and landings smoother. I had two quad jumps planned, something none of my rivals would attempt, and for the first time I went into each of them with utter confidence.

The audience, subdued at first, was with me before the end, clapping, stomping, whistling. I rode their cheers, pumped with adrenaline as though we were all racing toward some simultaneous climax, and in the last minute I turned a planned double-flip, double-toe-loop into a triple-triple, holding my landing on a back outer edge as steadily as though my legs were fresh and rested.

The crowd's roar surged as the music ended. Fans leaned above the barrier to toss stuffed animals, mostly cats, onto the ice, and one odd flutter caught my eye in time for a detour to scoop up the offering. Sure enough, the fabric around the plush kitten's neck was no ribbon, but a pair of lavender panties. Still warm. It wasn't the first time.

Suli waited at the gate. I gave her a cocky grin and thrust the toy into her hands. Her expressive eyebrows arched higher, and then she grinned back and swatted my butt with it.

The scoring seemed to take forever. "Half of them are scrambling to figure out if you've broken any actual rules," Johanna muttered, "and scheming to make up some new ones if you haven't." The rest, though, must have given me everything they had. The totals were high enough to get me the bronze medal, even when none of the following skaters quite fell down.

Suli stuck by me every minute except for the actual awards ceremony, and she was right at the front of the crowd then. In the cluster of fans following me out of the arena, a few distinctly catlike "Mrowrr's!" could be heard, and then good-humored laughter as Suli threw an arm around me and aimed a ferocious "Growrr!" back over her shoulder at them.

Medaling as a long shot had condemned me to a TV interview. The reporter kept her comments to the usual inanities, except for a somewhat suggestive, "That was quite some program!"

"If you liked that, don't miss the exhibition tomorrow," I said to her, and to whatever segment of the world watches these things. When I added that I was quitting competition to pursue my own "artistic goals," she flashed her white teeth and wished me luck, and then, microphone set aside and camera off, leaned close for a moment to lay a hand on my arm. "Nice costume, but I'll bet you'll be glad to get it off."

Suli was right on it, her own sharp teeth flashing and her long nails digging into my sleeve. The reporter snatched her hand back just in time. "Don't worry," Suli purred, "I've got all that covered."

Don't expose yourself like that! Don't let me drag you down! But I couldn't say it, and I knew Suli was in no mood to listen.

I was too tired, anyway, wanting nothing more than to strip off the unitard and never squirm into one again, but Suli wouldn't let me change in the locker room. Once I saw the gleam of metal she flashed in her open shoulder bag—so much for security at the Games!—I followed her out and back to our room with no regret for the parties we were missing.

The instant the door clicked shut behind us she had the knife all the way out of its leather sheath. "Take off that medal," she growled, doing a knockout job of sounding menacing. "The rest is mine."

I set the bronze medal on the bedside table, flopped backward onto the bed, and spread my arms and legs wide. "Use it or lose it," I said, then gasped at the touch of the hilt against my throat.

"Don't move," she ordered, crouching over me, her hair brushing my chest. I lay frozen, not a muscle twitching, although my flesh shrank reflexively from the cold blade when she sat back on her haunches and slit the stretchy unitard at the juncture of thigh and crotch.

"Been sweating, haven't we," she crooned, slicing away until the fabric gaped like a hungry mouth, showing my skin pale beneath. "But it's not all sweat, is it?" Her cool hand slid inside to fondle my slippery folds. It certainly wasn't all sweat.

Her moves were a blend of ritual and raw sex. The steel flat against my inner thigh sent tongues of icy flame stabbing deep into my cunt. The keen edge drawn along my belly and breastbone seemed to split my old body and release a new one, though only a few light pricks drew blood. The rip of the fabric parting under Suli's knife and hands and, eventually, teeth, was like the rending of bonds that had confined me all my life.

Then Suli's warm mouth captured my clit. The trancelike ritual vanished abruptly in a fierce, urgent wave of right here, right now, right *NOW NOW NO-O-W-W-W-W!* Followed, with hardly a pause to recharge, by further waves impelled by her teasing tongue and penetrating fingers until I was completely out of breath and wrung out.

"I thought I was supposed to be storing up energy," I told her, when I could talk at all.

"Jude, you're pumping out enough pheromones to melt ice," Suli said, "and I'm not ice!"

It turned out that I wasn't all that wrung out, after all, and if I couldn't talk, it was only because Suli was straddling my face, and my mouth was most gloriously, and busily, full.

The chill kiss of the blade lingered on my skin the next day, along with the heat of Suli's touch. I passed up the chance to do a run-through of my program, which didn't cause much comment since it was just the exhibition skate. Johanna, who knew what I was up to, took care of getting my music to the sound technicians with no questions asked.

There were plenty of questioning looks, though, when I went through warm-up muffled in sweats and a lightweight hoodie. Judging from the buzz among my fans, they may have been placing bets. Anybody who'd predicted the close-cropped hair with just enough forelock to push casually back, and the unseen binding beneath my plain white T-shirt, would have won. The tight blue jeans looked genuinely worn and faded, and from any distance the fact that the fabric could stretch enough for acrobatic movement wasn't obvious.

It was my turn at last. Off came the sweats and hoodie. I took to the ice, rocketing from shadows into brightness, then stopped so abruptly that ice chips erupted around the toes of my skates. There were squeals, and confused murmurs; I was aware of Suli, still in costume from her own performance, watching from the front row.

Then my music took hold.

Six bars of introduction, a sequence of strides and glides— and I was Elvis, "Lookin' for Trouble," leaping high in a spread eagle, landing, then twisting into a triple-flip, double-toe-loop. My body felt strong. And free. And *true*.

Then I was "All Shook Up," laying a trail of intricate footwork the whole length of the rink, tossing in enough cocky body-work to raise an uproar. Elvis Stojko or Philippe Candeloro couldn't have projected more studly appeal. When my hips swiveled— with no trace of a feminine sway—my fans went wild.

They subsided as the music slowed to a different beat, slower, menacing. "Mack the Knife" was back in town: challenge, swagger, jumps that ate up altitude, skate blades slicing the ice in sure, rock-steady landings. Then, in a final change of mood, came the aching, soaring passion of "Unchained Melody." I let heartbreak show through, loneliness, sorrow, desperate longing.

In my fantasy a slender, long-haired figure skated in the shadows just beyond my vision, mirroring my moves with equal passion and unsurpassable grace. Through the haunting strains of music I heard the indrawn breaths of a thousand spectators, and then a vast communal sigh. I was drawing them into my world, making them see what I imagined…. I jumped, pushing off with all my new strength, spun a triple out into an almost effortless quad, landed—and saw what they had actually seen.

Suli glided toward me, arms outstretched, eyes wide and bright with challenge. I stopped so suddenly I would have fallen if my hands hadn't reached out reflexively to grasp hers. She moved backward, pulling me toward her, and then we were skating together as we had so often in our private predawn practice sessions. The music caught us, melded us into a pair. Suli moved away, rotated into an exquisite layback spin, slowed, stretched out her hand, and my hand was there to grasp hers and pull her into a close embrace. Her raised knee pressed up between my legs with a force she would never have exerted on Tim. I wasn't packing, but my clit lurched with such intensity that I imagined it bursting through my jeans.

Then we moved apart again, aching for the lost warmth, circling, now closer, now farther…the music would end so soon… Suli flashed a quick look of warning, mouthed silently, "Get ready!" and launched herself toward me.

Hands on my shoulders, she pushed off, leapt upward, and hung there for a moment while I gripped her hips and pressed my mouth into her belly. Then she wrapped her legs around my waist and arched back. We spun slowly, yearningly, no bed, this time, to take the weight of our hunger. And then, as the last few bars of music swelled around us, Suli slid sensuously down my body until she knelt in a pool of scarlet silk at my feet. She looked up into my eyes, and finally, gracefully and deliberately, bowed her head and rested it firmly against my crotch as the last notes faded away.

An instant of silence, of stillness, followed, until the crowd erupted in chaos, cheers and applause mingling with confusion and outrage. TV cameras were already converging on our exit. I pulled Suli up so that my mouth was close to her ear; her hair brushing my cheek still made me tingle.

"Suli, what have you done? What will—?"

She shushed me with a finger across my lips. "Sometimes, if you can't stand to be left behind, you *do* have to jump without knowing exactly where you'll land."

So I kissed her right there on the ice for the world to see. Then, hand in hand, we skated toward the gate to whatever lay beyond.

YOU ARE A FULL MOON WITHOUT CLOUDS

Pamela Smiley

Chiang Mai was my city. I claimed it, even though I was hardly the first. The Rose of the North, nestled in the foothills of the Himalayas near the notorious Golden Triangle and its opium, had slid through history under siege: the Lanna Kingdom, Burmese invasions, American anthropologists, tourists, and ex-pats. The joke during the sixties was that every hill tribe family had its own resident anthropologist, so anxious were the Pentagon and CIA to track movement on the Ho Chi Minh Trail. Traces of *Chiang Mai's* siege identity remained in the sagging red brick wall and moat around the old city, in the Burmese-featured demons on temple murals, in the stories of the lion-faced Buddha who controls the rains being plastered over to protect him from marauding Burmese armies and then forgotten for hundreds of years until, during a move, the painted plaster cracked and the gold glinted within.

Chiang Mai was mine—and like many a fabled seductress, she gave of herself without ever really giving herself. I knew

Chiang Mai's smell—fried hot peppers and backed-up sewer gas. I knew her labyrinthine streets in the *Warorut* Market where anything and anyone could be bought. I knew where to go for a great cup of coffee, a three-mile run, the latest ex-pat gossip, and email connections. I knew the children who sold leis of jasmine in the nighttime streets, the bar girls, the saffron-robed monks, the pretty young boys, and I knew her soul: *Doi Suthep*, the Buddhist *wat* floating as serenely above the complex street life as the lotus floated above the muck in which it was rooted.

Now, as we pulled into the *Chiang Mai* train station, I wondered if my falling in love would change my relation to *Chiang Mai*. Superficially, things remained the same. Passengers scrambled for luggage, children and boxes, in reverse of their boarding. Rue, at my side, stretched to get the overhead bags and that made all the difference. Watching others make such gestures of intimacy and common purpose was not to feel the warm connectedness of performing them yourself.

"You wait with the luggage and I'll go get a *tuk-tuk* for us," I said to Rue, relishing that we were in this together.

Out on the street at the taxi stand, the light changed and traffic surged forward, waves of motorbikes vibrating like cicadas back home in Wisconsin. So many people, so many directions, so many desires—*Chiang Mai* was not about to be easily impressed just because I'd fallen in love.

Across the street from the taxi stand, an old Chinese woman, so old it didn't seem possible to fit any more wrinkles on her face and hands, struggled with a walker and headed toward us. She moved steadily forward, lifting her walker, taking a step, another step, lifting her walker, taking a step.

The milling men and traffic paid no attention to her. Young men on motorcycles snaked through lines of stalled cars, passing on the sidewalk to avoid her. I sprinted to the old woman.

"Grandmother," I said. "Let me help you."

She didn't seem surprised, though I'd never seen her before.

"Is your husband back from America?" she asked.

On which of the 108,000 levels of reality were we conducting this conversation? Not one I knew.

"No." I didn't elaborate since the particulars of my single status usually elicit nothing but pity from Asian women.

"I think you bought my song," she chuckled, as if we were in collusion to outwit the rest of the world.

A *tuk-tuk* separated itself from the pack of traffic. The driver hopped out and bustled Grandmother's walker and Grandmother herself into the back. But before she drove off, Grandmother squeezed my arm and said what she wanted me to hear. "The song is silent, daughter. Let passion bring it to life."

Perhaps *Chiang Mai* wasn't as insensitive to my being in love as I had thought.

The next *tuk-tuk*, for Rue and me, dropped us off at the Suan Doi House, hidden in an out-of-the-way *soi* off *Heuy Kau* Road on the university side of town. A little slatted bridge crossed from the parking area to the garden for which the hotel was named—gravel walks wending through plants and fountains with koi, a gazebo, and a treetop meeting house—all compacted within the space of an everyday hotel lobby

"*Sawadee-kah*," I called into the greenery.

"*Sawadee-kah*," a hoarse croak responded, one of the myna birds caged here and there in the garden. Its yellow-ringed eye looked at me, turned ninety degrees and looked again with the candor of a creature not intending to be fooled.

"*Sawadee-krap, Ajaan Picara*," Kuhn Witchera, the hotel owner, *weied* me with a charming unfocused smile that was the Thai ideal of *jai yen*, cool heart. "Welcome back to my hotel."

"*Kahp-kuhn kah*," I *weied* in return. "Do you have a room for me and my friend, Rue?"

He disappeared behind the reception desk and reappeared with a heavy key chain with *10* embossed in antique black against the worked tin. We followed him up along the balcony, leaving our shoes on the mat outside room 10.

Once Witchera closed the door behind him, Rue threw herself on the pink-lace canopied bed and patted the sheet next to her.

"How 'bout we take a little nap before we go out?" she asked with a knowing smile.

All my heady excitement crumbled. With awkward self-consciousness, I slid my bottom from the edge of the bed to where her hand lay.

"Here, let me spoon you," she suggested, and I rolled on my side and pushed the length of my back against her. Her arms folded tightly around me, and she tucked her chin into the hollow of my neck as if we were designed to fit together.

She smelled like Rue—even in the short time we'd been intimate, I came back to her smell as to an old comfort, the warm body smell of sweat and traces of metal, rather than soap or deodorant or toothpaste.

As Rue's breathing grew more regular and the strength of her grip relaxed, I squeezed my eyes shut.

"Rue is here," I whispered, ending my conversation with the Chinese grandmother. A month ago I hadn't known Rue existed, and now an abundance of possibilities beyond anything I could ever have known or imagined opened to me because of her.

But even in the midst of all this abundance, I felt a nagging fear, the part of love no one ever mentions. What had been found could also be lost. I had done nothing to set love in motion and had no experience of how to keep it from slipping away. It was a complete gamble. Everything depended on Rue patting the sheets next to her, on her saying "There's energy between us," on her leaning forward and marking my face with her curls.

I'll take her to Doi Suthep, I bargained with fate as Rue's soft breath feathered the back of my neck. *If this hits a snag, I'll hightail it to the* Karen *village and pretend Rue and the train ride never happened.*

Doi Suthep has always been a touchstone for me. Familiarity did not stale its charms. I liked everything about the *wat*, from the way it stood watch on *Chiang Mai* from the mountaintop to the fireworks blooming in the darkness during *Sokran,* the water goddess festival. I liked the monks chanting, and seeing the gold of the *cheddi* against the forest green from my bedroom window.

I even liked the legend of how it came to be. When the Buddha died of food poisoning, he asked that his remains be distributed wherever his teachings were practiced. A bone was sent to the King of the Lanna people in *Chiang Mai* and when the casket was opened, a miracle happened—two bones where there had been one.

The King vowed to put the second bone on the back of a white elephant and wherever that elephant rested, the King would build a *stuppa*. The elephant climbed the mountain, breaking through the forest where monkeys and tigers lived and humans seldom ventured, until it reached the site where the *wat* now stands. There, the elephant turned three times in a circle, a clap of thunder sounding in the cloudless blue sky, and dropped down dead.

So the legend goes.

A red *silor,* instead of a white elephant, shuttled Rue and me and four other tourists up ten miles of switchbacks to *Doi Suthep,* to the bottom of the three-hundred-step *naga* staircase.

The water snake, the *naga*, who so badly wanted to follow the Buddha that he disguised himself as human, undulated up the mountain, green tile scales and multiple heads. At the top of the stairs, plaster archways painted with warrior guardians kept out the demons and allowed the rest of us into the outer, this-worldly ring of the *wat*. *Doi Suthep* replicated the universe in its mandala design. Circles and squares inside one another spiraled to the sacred center, which for the *wat* was the *stuppa* containing the collarbone of the Buddha and for the universe was Mt. Meru.

"My last girlfriend before Nila—Rachel—told me I was looking for God." Rue did her version of combing her hair—raking her fingers through the curls, ending in a final upward tug.

"Well, if you can't find God here, there's not much hope," I joked, brushing the line of temple bells to alert the spirits to our presence—or to scare them away, depending on your world view. In this outer ring of the *wat*, all the faithful's this-world concerns were addressed: the happy Buddha with fat belly and bag of gold, the gold-leafed statue of the monk who built the road to the *wat,* the gold-ribboned *bodhi* tree, a blue-headed Ganesh, a coffeeshop, *bikkhanu* nuns with shaved heads and white robes renting skirts to cover tourist's bare arms and legs and selling bundles of lotus buds, yellow candles and joss sticks. Animism, Hinduism, ancestor-worship, consumerism, globalism, and Buddhism all represented.

I exchanged thirty *baht* for two bundles of lotus buds and joss sticks, earning a smile from the tiny old *bikkhanu* who'd devoted the end of her life to the Buddha, and led Rue by the hand through the gates and into the inner courtyard.

The cold marble beneath my feet, the smell of incense, the sound of the temple bells hanging from the rafters, each with a prayer written on its clapper to be carried by the wind to the

Buddha's long-lobed ears: every sense was fed by the *wat* but none as powerfully as the sight of the gold *stuppa* at the center. The *cheddi* rose like a giant child's set of gold-plated blocks, stacked in a pyramid touching the sky.

I dipped the white-and-green lotus bud in the brass cauldron and touched it to my forehead, shoulder, and heart. Then I blessed Rue the same way.

"What's that line-up all about?" Rue asked, pointing to the corner.

"It's the monk-blessing where he—or his assistant since he can't touch women—ties a white string around your wrist to keep all your souls together lest one get lost while traveling and you become estranged from yourself."

"We'd better do that, don't you think?" Rue nodded seriously. "No sense in risking losing my soul when I'm already in danger of losing my heart."

I laughed, knowing I wasn't allowed to take her words as anything more than a pretty turn of phrase, but my heart skipped.

We got our souls tied together, kneeling in front of the monk as he chanted and sprinkled water on our bowed backs. We wore the strings until, bleached and rotted by sun and sweat and chlorine, they broke. I tucked mine in a box where I kept the poem Rue wrote for me. I don't know what she did with hers.

"The only thing we haven't done is to have our fortune told," I said.

The clatter of bamboo sticks came from across the *wat*, from a room that was empty save for sticks, a bamboo cup, and a rack on the wall with fortunes printed on newsprint.

We knelt and Rue picked up the cup. She closed her eyes, bowed her head and then peeked at me with one eye. "Okay? Now?"

"Go for it."

She never told me the question she asked the sticks. I asked one of my own because I needed the sign from *Doi Suthep* I'd bargained for back in room number 10.

From out of the clump of sticks, one fell as she shook the cup up and down: number eleven. I took a slip of newsprint from number eleven on the cubbyhole rack.

"Number eleven," I read. *"You are the full moon without clouds. Your voice will sing of the moon's fullness, a song already paid for but not yet sung. Any lawsuit will end in your favor. Avoid all ventures that require new clothes."*

For a few extra *baht,* the *silor* took us back down the mountain and dropped us off at the Amari Rincom hotel, where the wealthy people stayed. On the intersection of *Huey Kau* and *Nimmenhamen* Road, the Amari was conveniently close to our hotel and the secondhand market where Kuhn Ji cooked some of the best *pak boohn* in the city. The secondhand market—maybe because of its tattoo-parlor booths and puppies for sale—was a place upwardly mobile Thais—"High-so" in Thai-English slang—forbade their children to hang out. I considered it—and Kuhn Ji's *pak boohn*—my insider's secret.

Kuhn Ji cooked over a butane flame stove he carted in on his motorbike every evening. His wife, Unchalee, took care of everything else—waiting tables, washing dishes, collecting money, and refreshing her signature red lipstick.

When he cooked, Kuhn Ji played to the drama. Flames—ten inches at least—leapt as if through sorcery as he tossed oil into the pan at a vertical angle. Then garlic. Peppers. Morning glory vines. Every ingredient sizzled as it hit the pan, and in less than three minutes, he turned off the gas, poured the *pat boohn* on a plate of rice Kuhn Unchalee held out to him, and handed me dinner.

"*Ajarn Picara! Swadee-krap!*" He tipped his invisible hat.

"Wow," Rue said, eyes wide. "Can he do that again?"

"Oh, yeah," I bragged with a giddy willingness to make the whole world sparkle in its best dress. "Kuhn Ji can do anything."

We shared the dinner and a *Chang* beer Kuhn Unchalee dug from the chipped ice in the cooler. I poured for each of us and, with my finger, traced one of the water beads on the brown bottle to where it pooled into a ring on the red Formica.

"To us." Rue raised her glass and winked at me.

Tonight was our first real night together, and I was nervous. I couldn't count on tricks like the magic of *Doi Suthep* or full moon without clouds or the secondhand market. But I was excited, too. Being with her...tonight, in the canopied bed with its velcroed lace...tonight...our bed...our first real night together.

My mind blanked. We'd run through the basics, the stuff we hadn't covered in chitchat—she'd sold her business and was giving herself a year to decide on the next part of her life; I taught at a small Midwestern college; she drove a 1979 Volvo, I my grandmother's red Acclaim; she lived in an urban cabin on Capitol Hill in Seattle, I in a brick salt-box in blue-collar Wisconsin.

Pumped-up music from the other vendors, traffic from *Huey Kau* Road, and behind all of them, the noise of frogs and insects looking for one another in the dark filled our conversational lull. Rue tried to lock eyes with me as I provoked a second bead to run its jagged course down the bottle.

"Time for bed?" Rue raised her eyebrows and twisted her mouth into a straight line of mock sternness.

I didn't trust myself to do anything but nod. We pushed back our stools and walked chaste as nuns until we got to the shadows of our own *soi*, where Rue took my hand. I kissed her with frogs vibrating in the background and the whole world humming with romance.

In our room, despite the heat, I dragged a long nightgown out of my rucksack as Rue showered. All those beers and I was still stone sober. When Rue stepped back into the bedroom, a towel tied around her, drops of water beading on her shoulders and chest and all soft and warm and pink from the shower, I had to force myself to stop staring.

Rue came so close to me I could feel her body's warmth. She pinched a fold of fabric from my nightgown between her thumb and finger.

"Are you not attracted to me?" she asked in a deep voice. "Or just shy?"

I swallowed. "Shy," I breathed.

"Ahh," she sighed, gathering a fistful of my nightgown in her hand and pulling me toward her, "I can take care of that."

FIRSTS

Hannah Quinn

The first time I met her, it wasn't like fireworks or thunderbolts or anything, the earth didn't move, there were no helpful portents to alert me to the momentousness of the occasion. I wanted her, of course I did, and not just because I was going through a frustrating dry spell. There was something about her—a kind of charming, disarming self-awareness; a boyish dashing charm, mischief in her eyes. It was as if you couldn't tell whether she was just laughing, or laughing at you, but there was nothing cruel about it. Impish, I suppose, but with a maturity that suggested she had a plan, that she knew exactly what she was doing. We flirted that night, exchanged stories of exes, established positions in some unspoken way. I didn't get her that first time, and of course that made me want her even more.

The first time she contacted me was bewildering. Initially oddly irritating, it beguiled and excited me too. I felt myself being drawn forward into something unknown. Dark water, like I couldn't see the bottom and I didn't know if she could either.

I wrote back; tried to take control of the exchange, steer myself into the realms of safety, of what I thought I knew—of sex and secrets and sordid affairs. Games I thought I knew the rules of. I knew a bit more about her then, knew she was with someone, and being single, pretended I had the upper hand.

The first time she phoned me I was dazed. It felt like moving forward, like more commitment than I was ready for and at the same time there was something charmingly old-school about it. There was also more potential to slip up, to be seen, to get trapped, than with the well-crafted texts and emails that were my safe zone. She wrong-footed me there, caught me off guard. Made me late too, and made me get on the wrong train. Captivated by her too-soon familiarity, her disregard for the rules of engagement, I was drawn on, drawn in.

The first time she came to see me, the first time she kissed me, was pleasure and pain like I'd never known. She kissed me, she left me, she possessed me. I didn't know it then, when the door closed, but the dark water was lapping at my knees. That was the first time I fucked myself and thought of her. If I could go back now, taking what I know, that would be the point around which everything revolves, that moment, that instant, that kiss, that kitchen, that hallway, that door. Certainly I didn't know it then, or at least couldn't see it, and I wish I had. I continued my smoke-screen dalliances with my single life, drank, talked, smoked, laughed, kissed, fumbled, heady on my own decadence and denial. Denial that it mattered, that she had any bearing on my life, that I even thought about her going home to someone else. Denial of the dark water, of the precipice, of the threat.

The first time she fucked me was filthy and furious and glorious. We'd both snuck out of work and that stolen daytime hour was all the more filthy and sweet for it. We didn't take our clothes off and I refused to let her in the bedroom. It was all about my boundaries, still pretending I could avoid the dark water, that it hadn't engulfed me. I carried her with me then though, as I went through my day, scratched and bruised and fucked and elated and astounded. It was physical and necessary and triumphant. It was the appetizer, and it left me wanting; it was as if we both knew it had to be done like that, just there and just then, before we could truly start. And by then, I knew we would, that it was inevitable.

The first time she stayed over, we went to bed. Sure, I tried to play it cool—canceled on her first, then relented; had some drinks, a little bit of weed; talked, reveled in the fact that we had all night, our abundance of stolen time. I couldn't stand the anticipation, the nerves, the wanting. Just being there, knowing that I was going to be with her, inside her, all over her—that I had her, that the door was locked and neither of us was going anywhere till morning. That was the first time I fucked her, saw her, found her, knew her. Giddy with the sight of her, the smell of her, the taste and feel of her. The silksaltsweetsweat closeness of her. I was intoxicated, addicted, exhilarated but never sated. We didn't sleep that night.

That first morning I was unrecognizable to myself, I was transformed by her, by the joy, despair, pleasure, pain, filthy sweetness; by the physicality of it all, betrayed by my flesh and hooked. My body dragged me into the world that day, made a convincing pretence of being present, said the right things at the right time to the right people but all the time craving, desperate, thirsty for her, for experience, for touch, for taste. I was reduced, stripped down, naked. I was flesh and need and want with no human finesse. I let my life carry on around me but withdrew, snuck off, allowed myself to wallow, to want, to dream, and to fantasize. She had me. I was broken and there was no going back.

The first days, weeks, months we pushed our bodies to their limits. We tended to our basic needs just to enable ourselves to keep going, to push farther, harder, more, desperately trying to slake our thirst for each other. It was primal, animal, and it was survival. We soon found the answers—how much sleep you actually need to hold down a job, how long you can avoid the world before it pushes back in; how many scratches, bruises and bites you can hide; how far from human you can travel in dedicated, determined pursuit of each other.

The first time we really made love, I died. Looked into her eyes looking into my eyes and fell from orbit. Lost, released, untethered, sobbing, and taken. I admitted it then, that I loved her, and we transformed again, became explorers, discoverers, mapping out paths across each other's body, learning, knowing, guessing, trying. We charted our lives around each other, points in common, leagues apart. Reveled in the knowing and the not knowing, the discovery of our selves, mirrored in each other. We awoke then, at some unacknowledged point, and rejoined the world a little, finding it changed in our absence, softer and more welcoming. Found that the truths we had long held were merely places to stand and created our own place to stand together.

The first time we acknowledged what we were, the power and the beauty of it, I cried. We found ourselves somehow, somewhere in the moment, crackling, bright, crisp, pure—like crystal, as though if we held it too tight it would shatter. I looked at her then and saw all that we were and are and will be—the dark water, the secrets, the need, the want, the animal, and the vulnerable. Everything and nothing and now and forever.

SOAKED

Erin O'Riordan

The air was thick with electricity. I'd been out once that morning for my early philosophy class. Since then, the little bit of sunlight I'd seen as I crossed campus had evaporated, and it was hammering rain. Rain bounced off the tennis courts like a pianist's fingers off the keys.

I love a thunderstorm. The vibrations of the thunder, the palpable crackle of the lightning, all excite me, making me feel alive. Rain is romantic, but a thunderstorm is erotic. I live for a good, hard, soaking thunderstorm.

At the opening chords of "Jenny (867-5309)," I turned off the radio. The '80s flashback show was too lame for the gorgeously dreary day this was shaping up to be. Besides, it was time to go to class again anyway.

I heard the first roll of thunder as I neared Weiss Hall. It was also the last; the thunderstorm was not to be. Still, by the time I got inside Weiss, my entire body was soaked with rain. I slipped into the restroom to grab some paper towels. At least I could towel off my face and arms. By some miracle, she was there.

First thing this morning, when I should have been paying attention in philosophy, I'd been studying her instead. She was sitting next to Lucy DeLuca today. By any traditional standard, Lucy should be the more beautiful woman. Lucy is petite and feminine, with long red hair and neatly made-up fingernails. Granted, ink blue is not the most traditional of colors for a manicure, but still, her nails were neat. But she's too thin. Her face is skinny, and she has tiny little thighs. Bailey has very short hair, and she bites her fingernails. She has lovely round cheeks, even lovelier rounded thighs, and a deliciously round ass. She's athletic. Strong, not skinny. And I'm not attracted to Lucy at all, but I love Bailey.

And by some miracle, there she was, in the ladies' room, drying her soaking-wet hair with the automatic hand dryer. Her white T-shirt clung to her, and her blonde hair was matted down against her head. She looked like someone had tried to drown her, but she was still cute.

"Hi, Beck," she said.

"Hi, pretty girl."

She giggled. "Quit teasing me," she said. "I look like a drowned rat."

"Then you're the prettiest drowned rat I've ever seen," I said, reaching out to brush a strand of wet hair away from her eyes. She returned the favor, brushing drops of water from under my chin with a paper towel.

"You're so sweet," I said. She stood there in front of the mirror, smiling, and I saw my chance. I kissed her cheek, in a purely friendly-playful way. I watched her face to gauge her response.

She winked at me, then grabbed my hand. Looking around to make sure no one was looking, she pulled me into the last stall. She locked the door behind us.

"What are you doing?" I asked, laughing.

"Shh." She pulled me close to her and whispered, "I've been wanting to do this for a very long time."

Now she tells me, I thought as she pulled her wet T-shirt up over her head. She hung it on the hook on the door. She put her arms around me, grabbed the bottom of my T-shirt, and pulled it over my head.

"I don't quite understand," I said. My confusion was almost as strong as my urge to reach out and feel her damp skin, the skin I'd been dreaming about since last semester. Dreaming, and nothing more. I had always been afraid to make the first move. And now my dreams were coming true...although honestly, I'd pictured our first kiss taking place in a locale a little more romantic than the first-floor loo in Weiss Hall.

"You don't need to understand," she said softly. "Just feel." She backed me up against the door and brought her lips to mine. I put my hands on her shoulders. She had the softest skin I'd ever touched, softer than I'd dreamed. She kissed my neck, and the warmth radiated through my rain-drenched body. I couldn't help but make some slight noise, some little squeals of joy. Her fingers traced their way down my collarbone. Just as she was about to explore the outlines of my wet bra, we heard footsteps. Another girl in the bathroom.

Bailey pulled away, and just like that, it was over. We put our wet shirts back on. Bailey exited the stall. I stood alone for a moment, experiencing undreamt-of loss. So this is what they mean when they say that a taste of honey is worse than none at all.

And yet somehow, despite the frustration, my first kiss with Bailey was perfect. So sublime, so...imaginary.

The truth is, I got to Weiss Hall soaked by the rain, gave myself a perfunctory once-over with a handful of gritty, cheap paper towels, and went to my Religion and Psychology seminar.

I sat across the table (there's only one table in the classroom) from Bailey and dreamt.

Bailey was wearing a multicolored choker of trade beads, the one that matches what must be her favorite orange T-shirt, the one she wears at least once a week. Freud says that orange is the color of insanity. I drove myself insane dreaming of the moment my fingers would glide over those beads on their way down Bailey's neck, as my eyes took in the sight of Bailey wearing that choker, and nothing but.

I drove myself insane dreaming of how Bailey had looked the night before, at Sociology for Women's Studies Majors, our one evening class together. She'd come in late because of intramural basketball. She was slightly sweaty and totally cute, in a red button-down knit shirt, jeans that beautifully showed off the curve of her thighs, and dirty, barely there white sandals. I'd never looked at Bailey's feet before. Somehow I'd imagined big feet, like a guy in the NBA would have. But really, Bailey's got tiny girl feet, just like me. I've never been into feet, but if there were any toes I could worship, they would be Bailey's little piggies, with their chipped coat of shiny lavender nail polish. I could plant my lips on them as pilgrims kiss the toes of a stone Virgin Mary. Better still, a pagan goddess. Bailey is, after all, Aphrodite to me, a goddess I approach with a swollen clit and a heart swollen with pure love.

I couldn't tell you what Religion and Psychology was about that stormy day. To me, it was about Bailey Rose Hutchins.

I thought about her as I went home for spring break. I spent the week waiting tables (my summer job, always there when I need it) and secretly checking out customers with Bailey's short-short blonde hair, her laugh, her long legs. Even when I wasn't around her, I was obsessed.

The first day of classes after spring break, I again had Religion and Psychology in Weiss Hall. Philosophy had been called off, so I hadn't had any morning classes, unless you count aerobics. I had a good workout and came back up to my dorm room in the mood to dance. I turned on the radio and let the '80s flashback show blast.

All that dancing made me thirsty, though, and I was having so much fun I decided to have a beer from the back of my minifridge. And then another. And then another.

I felt fine at the time, but in retrospect, I realize that I was a little tipsy. Okay, so by the time I got to the Religion and Psych seminar, it was obvious to every girl in class that I'd had a liquid lunch. Lucky for me, Fate intervened, and Professor Huang was not there. Instead she left instructions: we were to decide on a class project for the following week. She left four options for us to discuss. I'm sure my classmates made a decision, and I hope they wrote it down for me, because I wasn't paying attention. My attention, as always, was reserved for Bailey.

As we got up to leave, Bailey put her hand on my shoulder. Warmth radiated through me. "Are you all right, Beck?" she asked me.

"I'm never all right when you're around, Bailey," I blurted out. Oh, would that this had been the end of the conversation. Alas, I went on. "I see you, and my stomach twists up in a knot. I can't eat. I can't sleep. I can't even listen to the radio anymore because, shit, every song's about you, and how I don't have you. I am totally fucking knocked out by you."

That may not be the exact verbiage. I don't know that I'm that coherent after three beers. My memory of Bailey's reaction to this is sketchy. (That's probably a good thing.) I was told afterward by someone who witnessed the incident that I said this quite loudly, and that the whole class heard me. I excused myself and went back to my dorm room for a short but fruitful nap before my acting class.

Later, I called Bailey's room to apologize for my outburst. I got the answering machine. I myself cannot live with other people, but Bailey—outgoing, athletic, artistic Bailey, the popular kid, my opposite—has three roommates. I left a message: "Hi, this message is for Bailey. Only for Bailey, all right? Because it's kind of personal. Bailey, this is Beck Levinsky, and I'm sorry about what I said in seminar today. I'm...just really sorry, okay?"

Afterward, I had horrible visions of Liz, Kaye, and Tina listening to it and cackling at my utter patheticness. But what could I do? The damage was done.

So, to take my mind off my mistakes, I grabbed a couple of books and headed over to the student center. I was delighted to find that it was set up for open mic night. Ah, a chance for someone else to be the center of attention and make a complete ass of herself. I ordered an extralarge cappuccino, got a decent seat, and read until the first act came on. Two girls with guitars began a set of Indigo Girls covers. In between the music and my studies, I was pleasantly lost outside my own head.

Midway through the second-to-last act (a large group of guys, questionably sober, attempting to harmonize on Boyz II Men tunes), I looked up from my abnormal psych book and there was Lucy DeLuca, clutching her philosophy text in her ink blue–tipped fingers. Lucy's a philosophy and women's studies double major.

"Hey, Beck," she said, "how's studying going?"

"Oh, great," I said.

I waited for her to follow up with, "Great, because I heard you totally lost it in a theology course and confessed your lesbian love for Bailey Hutchins," but she didn't. Instead, she said, "I'm about ready to head back to the dorms. Want to walk with me?"

I shut my book. "Okay," I said. In truth, I hadn't been ready to go home yet. The open-mic performances had energized me, the way aerobics and the flashback radio show had earlier. Only now I was hyped up on sugar and caffeine instead of depressed by alcohol.

So, as Lucy and I started across the quad, I had a mad idea—I was going for a swim in the fountain at the center of campus. The night was warm and muggy, and I was overdressed in my jeans, so why not?

"Come on," I said, throwing my books.

"Where are you going?" Lucy dropped her backpack where I'd dropped mine—far enough from the fountain to be out of splashing range.

"Into the fountain!" I raced toward the center of the quad.

"No!" Lucy shouted. "You know we aren't allowed to play in the fountain. The sign says so. Besides, the bottom is all dark and slippery and icky."

"I'll be careful," I assured her. I already had one sneaker in the fountain. I almost slipped, momentarily thrown off guard by the shock of the cold water. I caught myself, then brought the other foot in. "It's cold, Lucy, but it's very refreshing. Come on in!"

Lucy shrugged, sighed, and stepped gingerly into the fountain. "There," she said. "Now we've played in the fountain. Can we go home now?"

I whooped with glee. "I'm having fun!" I let the fountain's jets spray me. My wet hair fell in my eyes, making a temporary curtain between me and the world.

"Breaking the rules isn't fun," Lucy said, deflecting the spray from her own face with her hands. "It's just a bad idea."

I deliberately splashed her, right across the front of her pink flannel shirt. "Which course taught you that?" I splashed her again. "Ethics?" Splash.

"It's common sense," she said. She waded back over to the edge and stepped out. Just then, a security guard began shouting at us. I could tell she was security by her walkie-talkie. Her red jacket made her look more like a movie theater usher.

"What do you two think you're doing?" The security guard pointed at the No Swimming, Wading or Diving sign. "Can't you read?"

I flicked a green penny off my shoe as I joined Lucy on dry land. "I'm sorry, ma'am," I said. "I know we shouldn't have been in there. I was just hot, and the fountain was cool. I told my friend to do it."

The security guard rolled her eyes, but overall, her face was kind. "Go on back to your dorm now," she said, "and stay out of the fountain. It *is* a memorial to the school's founders, you know. Have some respect for the dead."

"Yes, ma'am," I said again. "I'm sorry." I wasn't.

As the security woman walked away, Lucy said, "What course teaches you to jump in fountains?" She rung out her red ponytail. "I didn't know there was a course called Misdemeanors."

I smiled. "I just want to live my life with passion," I said. "I want to make mistakes and take the consequences for them."

"Oh, so that's what this is about."

"Oh, so you heard about my outburst in Religion and Psych after all."

"It's a small campus and news travels fast." She had that right.

I spilled my guts. It's a lot harder when you haven't just slammed three beers. "I told Bailey that I'm crazy about her, in front of an entire multidisciplinary seminar." That was only twelve people, but still. "Bailey's a straight girl, and I made a pass at her in front of everyone. Why? Because I was drunk."

Lucy was aghast. "You were drunk, too?"

"Of course. I can keep my feelings to myself when I'm sober. I'm not normally *that* uncool when Bailey's around."

She was thoughtful for one long, slow moment. Then she said, "What did she say? Did she say anything?"

"I didn't give her a chance," I said. We stopped in front of Lucy's dorm, and she said good night. She hugged me.

"Bailey will get over it," Lucy said. "Bailey is very cool."

Bailey is very cool was the mantra at the center of my universe, the precept on which I based my life. I didn't want her to get over it, though. I wanted Bailey to lie awake, thinking of my face as I lay awake thinking of her. In the morning when she woke, I wanted her thinking of me, and longing. I communicated none of this to Lucy, though. Instead, I said, "Whatever. It is what it is."

I took the long way back to my dorm, down the avenue. The wind blew the leaves of the trees gently, in eerie slow motion, giving a strange moving effect to the streetlights. Even my shadow flickered. I was looking down at it when I heard my name.

"Beck!" the voice said again. I turned around, expecting to see Lucy. Instead, there was Bailey.

She ran to where I stood dripping and befuddled. "Why are you wet?" she asked me.

"The school fountain attacked me," I said. "I was innocently minding my own business when it jumped me."

"Hmm," she said with a certain healthy skepticism. "Listen, Beck, I got your message."

"You did?" I said. "I mean, *you* got it, and not Liz or Kaye or Tina?"

"Well, Kaye was there, but she tactfully ducked into the bathroom before she heard anything…"

"Incriminating?" I offered. I gave my wet T-shirt a squeeze. Suddenly I felt very chilly. "Humiliating?"

"Beck, it's no big deal," she said. "Think of it this way—by the time we reach the age of twenty-two, three quarters of the population will have gotten drunk and blurted out their feelings to someone. You're not the only one."

"Thanks." I kicked a rock from the sidewalk.

"We're closer to my dorm than we are to yours," she said. "Why don't you come up? I'll get you some towels."

"No, thanks." I was thinking of how little I wanted to see Kaye, or Liz, or Tina, whether they'd heard my answering machine message or not.

Bailey seemed to pick that thought from my brain. "Are you sure? My roommates aren't around. Kaye's older brother took them to a bar in Rockport." She was rapidly advancing toward her building. Seemingly against my wishes, I was following.

"No kidding? How come you didn't go?"

"I have an art review in the morning. I'm here working on my unfinished drawings. I'm no good at hands and feet."

"Nobody is," I said, "except art majors, and that's why they're art majors."

"You could help me," she said. "You could take off your wet shoes and socks, and I could draw your feet."

I just laughed. We went up to her room, which was as dirty and colorful and funky as I'd imagined Bailey's room to be. Next to the art prints and clippings from fashion magazines on the walls, there was sports stuff. Bailey really loved the Detroit Pistons and the Red Wings. I knew it was her, too, because no one else was from Michigan. As a Blackhawks fan, I tried to hide my natural revulsion.

"Sit," she said, pointing to a futon under a loft bed.

"I'll leave a wet spot," I objected.

"Sit on that sweatshirt." She pointed to a gray lump on the floor. I picked it up, stretched it out, and sat on it. She grabbed some towels out of the closet and handed them to me.

Bailey's towels were orange. "Do you know what Freud says about the color orange?"

"It's the color of insanity," she said, "and it's my favorite color. What does that say about me?"

I didn't have an answer that I could put into words for her. I dried my hair with one of her orange towels and wrapped the other around my wet clothes. Next I took off my shoes and socks and shoved them to the side.

Bailey opened her cardboard portfolio, selected a drawing, and put it on the drawing board. She grabbed one of the artists' pencils that were scattered on the floor.

"Your feet are small," she said, "like mine."

I looked down at them and wondered when I'd last cut my toenails.

I don't know how long it took for her to complete the sketch, but when she was finished, she showed me the result. I didn't recognize the face in the portrait. I wouldn't have recognized my own feet if I hadn't watched her sketch them. They weren't perfect, but the drawing was better than what I could have done. And it was endowed with the magic of having been touched by Bailey's hands.

"Do you like it?" she asked me.

"Yes," I said. "You'll get an *A*."

And then it happened. Quick as a flash, Bailey's hands darted out and took mine. She pulled me to her, so that we stood in front of the futon, and she kissed me. Her soft lips were as warm and sweet as three shots of honey liqueur. I shivered.

"I knew I'd be wet the first time I kissed you," I said as I caught my breath. "This wasn't exactly what I had in mind."

I NEVER THOUGHT OF LOVE

Jacqueline Applebee

My girlfriend, Caitlin, once told me about the difference between British and American people. Apparently Americans think a hundred years is a long time, while the British think that a hundred miles is a long way. I'm very British. I live in London—Caitlin lives far away to the north. I see her once a month if I'm lucky. It isn't nearly enough, but I hope that one day my luck will change.

I wanted to tell Caitlin that I loved her when we lay together in bed on the first night of my visit. We'd been together for a while, but I'd never seen her home until then. Caitlin's mouth was open as I licked along her thighs. I was sure that if I kissed her lips, I would be able to breathe the words right inside her. Caitlin's eyes were open and staring at me as I swept my tongue over her, her hazel irises almost dilated to black. She looked more beautiful than anyone I had ever known. The words wouldn't come then, though I felt them against the back of my throat. They lay in wait, unwilling to rise. I kissed lower, licked her ankles and tickled her toes. She made a beautiful sound as she giggled for mercy.

I never thought I'd have feelings for a woman like Caitlin. She's smart, real book-smart, not like me at all. She's pale, she wears glasses, and even though she doesn't own any nerdy T-shirts, I know she'd look good in one. Her long wavy hair frames a beautiful serious face. I'd felt that hair wrapped around my brown fingers as I held her the next morning. I'd tugged on it as she came writing about on the bed, twisting the sheets as she moved. The first orgasm of the day was always a big one.

I've been in love before, but falling for Caitlin was different. Love soaked into my skin, flooding me. I never knew that I was drowning until my breath faltered whenever I lay in her arms.

Caitlin has five young kids. When she told me about them, my mind just boggled. I didn't know how I was going to deal with it. At first I made jokes and hid behind a pathetic shield to protect myself. I guess even back then I knew I would come to adore her and everyone she loved. Over time, I've found it impossible to picture Caitlin without a clutch of little, happy, pink faces surrounding her. It's not easy to say that I'm scared of that image. But I am. I'm terrified.

If you really want to know why, I'll tell you. There was once a time when there were children around me too. My nieces and nephews were a positive part of my life. I may not have given birth to them, but I raised those children as if they were my own. Unfortunately, my home was not a happy one. I lived in a place where threats and humiliation because of my sexuality were a part of everyday life. I used to be told that I was copying white people and their funny ways, that proper blacks are never queer and something must be wrong with me. My family caused me so much pain, it became unbearable. So I packed up and escaped without a word. I had to leave my children behind when I ran.

I left a part of myself behind too—the part that would make chocolate cupcakes on a whim, the part that would leave extra gooey mixture in the bowl, just so my kids could stick their little fingers in and wipe the bowl clean.

I was resigned that there would never be any other children in my life so I closed the hatch on possibilities. But life has a way of making impossible things real, in your face, and screaming for cartoons at six o'clock in the morning.

Caitlin's fourth child, Alan, hugged me at breakfast the next day. He clambered up onto a chair by the table to stretch his little arms around my waist. I pulled down a telephone directory and placed him on it, boosting him so he could see over the tabletop. He sang a nursery rhyme as he ate his cereal—I recognized it as one that I had sung to my nieces and nephews when they were toddlers. I stopped humming abruptly and sipped my strong black coffee instead.

Caitlin's youngest, Hazel, reached for a pair of scissors. I put them out of reach, hiding them on top of a tall bookcase.

"I hate you, Jenny!" she said with a pout. "Go away!"

I only smiled and said, "That's too bad, because I happen to think you're great." Hazel scowled at me, stuck out her tongue, and continued drawing with crayons. I cared for Hazel because I loved her mother. Plus Caitlin would go berserk if I let her little girl play with sharp objects.

Caitlin came down to breakfast dressed in her schoolteacher clothes, which for her meant lots of black, with a long skirt and a severe dark blouse. Her eldest child, Finbar, spilt milk over his school tie. Caitlin calmly rinsed out the cloth as he sat on the steps, helping Hazel to put on her shoes. From the corner of my eye I could see Kevin, the second eldest, as he dragged my big overnight bag into the kitchen. He rummaged around inside until he found the bar of dark, single-estate chocolate that I'd been saving for later. He grimaced as he took a bite.

"That's yucky!" he screeched, frantically scrubbing at his mouth. I laughed until my stomach hurt. Who knew that the shield I had created for myself would be dismantled by a beautiful teacher nerd and her crazy family? I should have been able to tell Caitlin that I loved her, because it truly was the way I felt.

"You know we don't have to do anything," Caitlin whispered later that evening, as if she could somehow sense my unease, my fear.

"It's just nice spending time with you," I replied like the liar I was. I wanted to stroke all over her skin, to feel everything she had. Her scent made me want to submerge myself in her. "We don't have to do anything," I continued nervously. Caitlin kissed me when I said that. Every ounce of my strength just fled once her lips touched mine. We made love for two hours straight.

I wanted to tell her that I loved her that night when her mouth was open in a soft circle. She was coming for the fourth or maybe fifth time. My fingers were deep inside her, touching, stroking. But her kids were asleep upstairs, so she kept the volume down as much as she could.

"Yes," she sighed as her muscles unclenched. I loved this strong, wonderful woman. Her head flopped back, and she released me from her clinch. My fingers stayed buried inside her heat. I never wanted to leave her. I wanted to make her scream into my shoulder. I wanted to hear her yell. My own mouth was shut tight. I didn't trust myself to utter anything, just in case I said too much. I knew what I wanted to say. I knew what I was feeling. But the words wouldn't come, not then. They were just waiting for me to exhale, to breathe out and give them life. I was a coward of the highest order.

Caitlin held me tightly as I fell asleep. I was scared, and my fear did not lessen as my eyes closed. I never thought of love, but now it was the only thing on my mind.

I sat in a London pub two weeks later. Caitlin's best friend, Penny, sat across a table from me. She kept on smiling at me, because she's a very perceptive woman. She could see that I was head over heels in love with Caitlin. Penny was getting over a cold that had made her lose much of her voice. She had told me croakily how it made her appreciate what came out of her mouth. She had been silent for most of the evening, but as the night wore on, her cheeks flushed red with wine. In the busy, noisy pub, I thought about all the things that I could say to Caitlin. I thought about telling her that I loved her, but without using any of those loaded words. Penny was ever the mind reader—she wriggled her eyebrows at me and then she picked up her bag and moved to leave. I walked her to the train station, quite unaware of anything but the memory of Caitlin's soft voice when she came, urgently panting against me.

Penny grinned as I hugged her. "Give Caitlin a call," she said with a rough voice, and then she ran for the waiting train. I opened and closed my mouth several times. I must have looked like a crazy goldfish, floundering on the station platform.

My fingers shook as I pressed the digits on my phone. The room closed in on me as the ring tone echoed through my ears. And then Caitlin picked up. Every single lightbulb in my home switched itself on. I squinted at the brightness of her voice.

"There's something I meant to say when I last saw you."

"Umm?" Caitlin sounded sleepy. I could hear Edward, the middle child, shouting in the background. It was after eight. He should have been in bed.

"I love you," I said quietly.

There were three seconds of silence, before my ears rang with the sound of high-pitched squeals and giggles.

"I love you," I repeated. "I love you, I love you." I took a breath. "I love you, Caitlin." My mouth would not be still. I started laughing like a crazy woman.

"I love you too, honey," she replied breathlessly after she stopped squealing. "Edward wants to talk to you."

I listened to Edward's excited voice as he told me that he had been given a gold star at school that day. Eventually he handed the phone back to his mother. I closed my eyes and pictured my nieces and nephews all smiling up at me, happy brown faces with wide toothy grins. A wave of sadness battled with the burst of joy, but I grinned into the telephone handset as I embraced the future. I loved Caitlin. This was something I never expected, but I could sense her love clear across the country. I stroked the handset, kissed the mouthpiece.

"I love you."

"When are you next coming up?" I could hear her voice suddenly close on the phone.

"Soon, honey." The miles between us melted as I spoke. "I'll come up next weekend. I love you." I suddenly felt very American—the weekend seemed so far away.

GIRLS AND
THEIR CARS

Renée Strider

I t started out as a joke—until things got a little out of control.

Carole and Janis each owned a Lexus. They were extremely proud of their cars and kept them in tip-top shape, always clean and shiny, motors purring, every bell and whistle working.

Carole was into old luxury cars. Her previous car had been a twenty-year-old Caddy. Her Lexus, which she'd had for about four years, was a shimmering, silver gray sedan. A very big sedan, one of the first from the early '90s, with a very big V-8 engine.

Janis preferred newer, more sporty cars. She was driving a Porsche when she decided she needed something "more practical." So, about a year ago, she'd bought an almost-new, gleaming black Lexus. A high-performance SUV that looked a little dangerous, at least in comparison with Carole's—let's face it—more sedate car.

Did Janis get her Lexus as a *nyah, nyah* to Carole? Their friends wondered. The two certainly competed in other areas and had done so from almost the day—well, night, at the lesbian bar—that Janis moved into town a couple of years back. Moved into Carole's territory, really, because Carole was the number one player in town and suddenly had to make room for another dyke who went after the ladies—the femmes—with just as much charm and enthusiasm, and with just as much success.

On the surface, the competition between the two was friendly, whether it was over women, pool, or cars. At the bar they would often discuss cars, especially their "Lexi," offering advice to each other and comparing specs till their friends would roll their eyes from boredom. But sometimes there was an edge to it—a sarcastic comment from Janis, a pointed joke from Carole—and those around them would widen their eyes or smirk knowingly.

That's how it went one midsummer Saturday night at Red Emma's. The whole crowd was there, including most of our heroes' past conquests. Nobody was completely sober, but nobody was really drunk, either. Both Carole and Janis were between girlfriends. That happened a lot—though not necessarily at the same time—a reluctance to commit being the *sine qua non* of playerhood.

It was close to midnight, and Carole was standing comfortably with her back against the bar, one knee bent, boot heel hooked over the brass rail near the floor. Her pelvis was tilted forward both for balance and for effect. In her right hand she hefted a bottle of beer while the thumb of the other hand stuck through a belt loop of her black jeans. She turned her head slightly and nodded as Abby, her companion at the bar, spoke to her, but her dark eyes were fixed on Janis.

Janis was sitting more or less across from her on a table with one thigh balanced on its edge, one black-and-white high-topped foot dangling and the other flat on the floor. She wore tight, faded blue denims and a loose white tank top that showed off her broad shoulders and tanned arms. Patty, one of the women sitting at the same table, said something to her and Janis bent her head to listen. She grinned and sat up, tipping her glass for a couple of big swallows. As she wiped her mouth with the back of her hand, she looked up and noticed Carole watching her.

"Hey, Janis. Car okay?" Carole drawled, lifting her bottle in Janis's direction. "I thought maybe she was stalled when I passed you today."

"Carole." Janis raised her beer, too, and straightened up, half-sitting, half-standing, with both feet now planted on the floor. "Was that you in your grandmother's car?"

Their friends snickered and they both smiled, if a little thinly.

"You guys should have a race," Abby said.

Carole snorted. "Wanna shoot some pool?" she asked Janis. "The table's free." Janis had beaten her two out of three games a few nights back, and Carole wanted payback.

They moved to the pool table at the back of the room, set their beers on a nearby table, and took a couple of cues off the wall, examining them carefully. Some of the other women gathered around to watch. Janis shoved a few coins in the tray, pushed, and the balls came rumbling out into the slot under the end of the table. Carole loved that sound and always imagined a network of dark tunnels under the tabletop through which the colorful balls raced at breakneck speed. She racked them up, solid and striped, into the triangle for eight-ball.

The lamp above the table turned Janis's short feathered hair to copper as she bent forward, sighting down her cue to break. Her top gapped open, partially revealing the swell of her breasts to Carole at the other end of the table. Carole quickly shifted her eyes away, but not soon enough to prevent her stomach from clenching and her face from reddening, to her total and utter consternation.

After the balls finished breaking, sinking one, Janis pocketed one more. Carole was still rattled, her cheeks hot, when Janis winked and stared at her pointedly, waiting for her to shoot. She failed to make a ball, but finally did get it together, and the score was four games to three for her by the time the bartender announced, "Time, ladies," and they called it a night.

Carole lived nearby, so she walked home as she usually did after an evening of drinking. What the fuck *was* that! Her reaction to seeing Janis's cleavage—pulse quickening, guts buzzing, and *blushing* for god's sake!—had been a shock. She'd never been attracted to another butch, yet she'd actually been aroused. She must really need to get laid. That's all it was, she decided. But what was that wink? She shrugged it off.

As she turned into her driveway, she admired the massive old Lexus glowing softly silver in the dim light of the streetlamp. Seeing it reminded her of Abby's tongue-in-cheek suggestion and the reactions in the bar. The rumors had flown.

"Hey, Abby said you're gonna have a race. When?" Jude had asked, as if it were a *fait accompli.*

And, as Carole was racking the balls up once more, this from Cindy who was very cute and one of Janis's exes: "Janis, can I drop the flag, pulleeze?"

Carole and Janis had mostly just grinned and brushed off the comments and questions and concentrated on their game. Their friends wouldn't let it go, though.

As Carole lay in bed going back over the evening, her thoughts lingered on the peculiar incident at the pool table. She drifted off in an erotic haze, her hand in Janis's shirt, reaching for a nipple. *No!* She came to with a start and sat up, heart racing. She breathed deeply to calm herself, then lay back down on her stomach and thrust her hand down, under her body, touching herself. She was *so* wet. She willed herself to think about somebody else, one of her current fantasies. She climbed on top of the gorgeous—and ultrafeminine—woman she'd been admiring at the gym, and took her hard, on a mat, pushing her fingers into her. Then she was licking her, all wet and hot, and the woman was writhing and moaning. In her imagination, even though Carole was going down on her, she was able to see the woman's face while she was coming. But as she jerked herself to a shuddering climax, the face dissolved into Janis's, and it was Janis arching against her and moaning with pleasure.

On Wednesdays—Hump Day—Red Emma's was usually pretty full right after work, as the women took advantage of the pub food served only on that day and on the weekend. That Wednesday was no exception. Carole and Abby were both sitting on bar stools eating and talking, occasionally glancing up at the mirror behind the bar to check out the room, when Abby said, "So what about that race, eh? C'mon, how about it? I'm serious. What a gas."

Carole shoveled a forkful of meat pie into her mouth, ignoring the question.

"You *know* you'd really like that SUV to eat your dust, not to mention its driver." Abby continued harassing her.

"Are you nuts? We'd get caught and they'd take away my car. Forget it." Nevertheless, she felt a tiny thrill, quickly suppressed.

Abby chewed thoughtfully. "No, you wouldn't—we wouldn't."

Carole regarded her best friend in the mirror. Uh-oh. Abby had the look that meant all the wheels were turning, and "no" would be a remote option when she finally marshaled her arguments.

Just at that moment, they saw Janis passing behind them. Abby whirled around and grabbed her arm, almost spilling the glass of beer in Janis's hand.

"Janis! C'mere. We're still talking about that race."

"No, we're not. I've been telling her no way," Carole growled. She hoped she sounded normal. Part of her mind was trying desperately not to think of her masturbatory fantasy of the other night.

"No way is right. We'd get caught and they'd take away my car," Janis said.

"What I said." Carole nodded solemnly.

"C'mon, Janis, you know you'd love to see that big old boat eat your dust," Abby urged. Indignantly Carole raised her eyebrows at her. "And I know just how you won't get caught." Abby smiled conspiratorially and lowered her voice. "You know my parents' farm north of town?"

Carole nodded. She'd been there many times.

"Well, it's huge, right?" Abby continued. "Lots of fields, mostly corn. Very tall corn. A couple of fields are fallow every summer, though. Just clover. You can see right across the field— no obstructions—so you could race around that. If there's one with cornfields all around, nobody would see us. And if it's at noon on a Sunday, nobody's around, anyway."

"What about the noise?" Carole asked, in spite of herself.

Janis just stared at them with round eyes.

"It's in the middle of nowhere, and nobody's gonna call the cops just because they hear a couple of engines revving."

"Are you guys nuts?" Janis found her voice. "I already said *no!*" She didn't sound as vehement as she might have, though.

"Hey, I haven't said *yes* either," Carole said.

But soon some of the others got involved in the discussion. They were all so high with enthusiasm that finally Carole and Janis got caught up in the excitement, too, and caved and said yes. Red Emma's buzzed with anticipation all that evening.

One woman suggested taking bets. Jude quashed that idea

pretty quickly. They could be in enough trouble already without adding illegal gambling to illegal racing.

"Listen up, everybody," Abby said in her take-charge, gravelly voice. "The race will be this Sunday. High noon. Do not advertise it, even as a joke. Don't talk about the race. If this gets back to us from outside this group, we'll have to cancel."

"But I was thinking of doing a poster for the bar. *Butch-on-Butch Street Racing,*" said Patty. Everybody laughed, but Abby glared at Patty. "Hey, I won't. I'm only kidding. Geez."

The butches in question both flushed as their glances locked. Neither seemed able to look away. Carole was dimly aware that Abby was watching them, fascinated, her eyes going from one to the other. Then somebody called to somebody else across the room, and the moment was over.

Carole's pulse was speeding. She could feel it in her throat. She refused to look at Abby as she passed by her to fetch a beer from the bar. Swallowing the cool liquid gratefully, she tried to slow down her breathing. Abby was at her side almost immediately.

"Hey, what's going on with you two?" she hissed.

"Nothing." Carole gave her a look that said, "Drop it or else," so Abby did, but she gave her a look in turn that said, "I don't believe you."

"Okay, so it's this Sunday, twelve o'clock," Abby said. "I'll find out where and look after all the details."

On Saturday morning Carole decided to check out the location of the pending race, maybe have a look at the road. She was familiar with the area and had no trouble finding the field Abby had described. She drove around it once. It measured about three-quarters of a mile on each side, flat as a pancake like the rest of the surrounding countryside. A shallow ditch ran along both sides of the road. No telephone poles, though, and the road was wide and paved. It was gray and roughly surfaced with age—rough was okay. It was in good condition, with no major cracks or potholes. The shoulders were only about a foot wide, but hard and dry with not much gravel. It didn't look as if traction would be a problem.

She stopped the Lexus and got out. A blast of heat hit her after the air-conditioning, even though the sun wasn't high yet. It shone into her eyes and reflected from the pavement, making her squint. The air was still, not the slightest rustle in the tall, dark green corn across the road, and the only sound the searing buzz of cicadas. Carole wondered where they were since she couldn't see any trees. Well, except for one that didn't count anymore. In the distance, a bare skeleton of a once-mighty elm stood alone in the middle of the field. She hadn't seen one of those in years, as most of them had died and been cut down long ago. Other than that, the field was empty, just a rock here and there. Abby was right; you could easily see from one side of the field to the other.

And that's why she could see a car coming even before it turned the corner onto the road where she was standing. Her guts contracted. A black Lexus SUV, shining in the sun. Janis.

Janis pulled up behind Carole's car and rolled down the window. "Wow, hot." They smiled at each other tentatively. "Checking things out?"

"Yeah," Carole said. "The road looks pretty good. Good surface. There's a ditch all around, though, on both sides."

Janis got out, examined the ditch, and looked out across the bare field. As usual, she was wearing faded blue 501s and a tank top. Carole admired her tight behind. She knew Janis worked out, just as she did. They often saw each other at the gym and would surreptitiously compare their buff physiques, or at least

Carole did. She was pretty sure Janis did, too. All part of the competition between them, of course. As Carole took in Janis's arms and shoulders, she suddenly felt even warmer and turned away, concentrating on the cornstalks across the road. She wiped her sweaty forehead with her arm, pushing back the damp brown curls, and with her other hand pulled her clammy muscle shirt high up on her back to get some air on her body. When she turned back, she caught Janis looking, her gaze fastened on Carole's bare skin, her lips parted. Their eyes met, and Carole had the same reaction again as at the pool table at Red Emma's.

A flash of scarlet broke their concentration when a red-winged blackbird landed on the fence in the cornfield.

"Well, I guess I've seen everything—uh, the road and all, so..." Carole cleared her throat and dug in a front pocket of her own faded Levis for her car keys.

"Okay, see you tomorrow. Should be fun," Janis said a little awkwardly and followed Carole to her car.

But as Carole reached for the door handle, she felt a hand clasping her bare upper arm. Shocked, she turned around, and they stared at each other for a split second before she was pushed backward against her car.

"I've been wanting to do this," Janis said hoarsely, grabbing her shoulders and shoving her leg between Carole's. Carole grunted with surprise, immediately aware of her wet crotch against the friction of Janis's thigh. Automatically she pushed her own thigh up against Janis's sex and, hands on Janis's ass, pulled her in harder. This was all wrong, but she didn't care. She was too turned on. Both women groaned when their lips and tongues came together, and Carole threw her head back and arched against Janis as Janis's hot wet mouth moved to her neck. The only sound besides their harsh breathing was the cicadas, but they didn't hear them.

When Janis wedged a hand between their bodies, fumbling with the buttons of Carole's fly, Carole suddenly came to her senses. "Un-uh," she said, and with a heave threw Janis off and switched positions. Janis laughed breathlessly as Carole pressed her back against the door with her whole body, rocking her thigh between Janis's as she moved her hips slowly back and forth. This time it was she who trailed her lips and tongue down Janis's throat toward the breasts she'd fantasized about.

"Oh, god," Janis said, and then, "I've never done this before," as she reached once more for Carole's buttons. This time Carole let her and moved back just enough to undo Janis's at the same time. As she touched smooth warm skin, Carole realized that she'd never unfastened a woman's fly buttons before either. Her femme girlfriends didn't wear Levi's with buttons.

Carole reached down Janis's belly to slick, swollen flesh at the same time as she felt a hand sliding through her hair and between her own labia. She leaned one arm against the car to keep from collapsing against Janis, leaving just enough room for their stroking. By now they were both moaning. Again they found each other's mouths, and their tongues glided together in the same rhythm as their fingers. After only a few seconds, Carole felt the first flutter of her muscles tightening into orgasm. She thrust farther into Janis's wet heat, and Janis cried out as they both came.

Limp and sweaty and still breathing hard, they leaned against the car side by side, hanging on to the door handles. The sun beat down on them, reflecting from the metal. With trembling fingers, they each did up their own buttons. They didn't look at each other. When Carole got her strength back, she got into her car and looked up at Janis through the open window. Janis's disheveled hair was a corona with the light behind her.

"You know I'm going to beat you, don't you?"

Carole blinked at the sudden change of direction. Janis's face was in shadow so she couldn't see it very well, but she sounded serious.

"Really. And why are you so sure?"

"Because I'm a better driver and my car's a lot faster."

Carole laughed. "Don't try to psych me out. It won't work. Not after this."

As she drove away, she watched Janis in the rearview mirror just standing there, looking after her, hands in her back pockets. Carole's hand on the steering wheel was damp. It must smell like Janis's cunt. She resisted the temptation to find out, not wanting to be aroused again, and wondered what the hell was going on with them. It was the heat, and they were both between women and extremely horny. It could have happened to anyone. She flushed and cringed a little inside. But with another butch?

The next day, Sunday, was even hotter. By noon it was already ninety-five in the shade; the sun was a weight pressing down on them. A small crowd had gathered. Carole counted eight cars (including both Lexi), three motorbikes, one scooter, and a bicycle, all parked well away from the actual raceway, the road encircling the empty field.

"Okay, listen up," Abby yelled in her official voice, raising a hand high. Then she said something into a squawking walkie-talkie. Apparently the woman at the other end was in the middle of the field under the dead elm, an observer with binoculars.

"The race will start in twenty minutes at the drop of the traditional green flag. It will begin here." Abby pointed at a white line spray-painted across the road. "It will proceed counterclockwise around all four sides of the field and end here at the drop of a rainbow flag." Everybody cheered and whistled at that. "For safety's sake, stay off the racetrack and well clear of the starting line and the finish. Competitors, come here, please."

Carole and Janis shuffled up to her. "A coin toss will determine your position. Heads or tails?" The drivers mumbled their choice, and Abby tossed a shiny coin spinning up into the air.

"Carole in the gray Lexus gets the inside; Janis in the black Lexus gets the outside. Now shake hands, and may the best woman win." They shook, grinning sheepishly, their hands clammy from heat and nerves; more cheering and whistling from the crowd.

As they sat in position in their softly purring cars, waiting behind the start line, Carole and Janis looked at each other for a long moment through the half-open windows. What passed between them at that moment Carole couldn't interpret, but somehow it felt good. She suddenly relaxed and wasn't nervous anymore. She stared straight ahead, focusing on the road, thankful that the sun was directly above and wouldn't shine in their eyes.

Five minutes to go. About fifteen feet up ahead, on the cornfield side of the road, Cindy appeared in pink halter top and short-shorts. She stood facing them, legs wide apart, holding up in one hand, as high as she could reach, what appeared to be a fluorescent lime green thong—the green flag for the start. There was no time to laugh. Carole glanced at the clock on the dash. Her heart rate picked up. Two minutes to go. They both revved their engines. She reveled in the sound—*rrrrum, rrrrum.*

Down came the green thong! They were off! Cindy was just a smudge in the landscape as they passed her, tires squealing, smelling of burning rubber, clouds of dust and grit following in their wake.

Carole stomped on the gas pedal. 0–60 in 7.9 seconds said the specs. She'd never tested that. It felt like 5 G's, forcing her backward against the seat. The SUV's specs said 0–60 in 6.8

seconds; she'd looked it up. She glanced over: neck and neck, and halfway down the first stretch. Two-thirds of the way, her speedometer read almost ninety mph. She sat in a tunnel of sound, wind whipping by the half-open windows, tires eating up the road, engines roaring. She had to slow down with the first corner coming up. The black SUV was pulling ahead. It must be that 0–60 in 6.8 takeoff, still an advantage in the first straightaway.

As Carole slowed down to forty to take the corner, Janis was almost a car length ahead of her. Janis took it wide, increasing the distance by another half car length as she zoomed over to the inside, cutting the gray car off but allowing Carole just enough room to stay in control directly behind her. They picked up speed again going into the second stretch. Relentlessly, Carole closed the distance between them to a half car length and then, just before running up the black car's bumper, she moved over to the outside, still closing.

Again they were abreast, burning up the road at almost a hundred. Same situation as in the first stretch, but with positions reversed. This time the gray car moved ahead, so gradually that they seemed to be standing still, side by side. Carole wasn't aware of the blur of the passing cornfield on her right, only of the straight road ahead and the black car on her left, which disappeared from her peripheral vision as she pulled ahead. Nearing the second corner, Carole was leading by at least a car length. Time to slow down again. Like Janis before, she took the outside corner wide, then swooped across to the inside, cutting Janis off but not giving her quite as much room as Janis had allowed. Maybe Janis hadn't decelerated as much when cornering.

Carole accelerated again, rapidly picking up speed down the third straightaway. Elated, she glanced in the rearview and right-side mirrors, needing to know the black car's exact position. She saw only dust. Puzzled, she looked again, losing speed without thinking. She knew the dust wasn't thick enough to hide a car close behind her.

Where was Janis? Fear clutched at her chest. She took her foot off the gas pedal and stepped hard on the brake, still glancing in the rearview mirrors. The gray car fishtailed wildly as she slowed it down to do a U-ie with one twist of the steering wheel. Big as it was, the old Lexus could turn on a dime. Carole raced back the way she'd come, peering apprehensively through the dust, eyes scanning the road, back and forth. After what seemed like eternity, suddenly, through the dust cloud, she saw the black car up ahead on her right, lying angled on its driver's side along the edge of the ditch. One wheel was still turning slowly and the front passenger-side door was sprung open.

"Oh, god, oh, god, no!" Carole's heart began to pound with dread. She skidded to a stop beside the SUV and jumped out. The car was about six feet wide, a little high to climb into from a ditch, especially if you added in having to climb over the seat, so she crawled frantically up the side of the hood to the open passenger door. She stuck her head in. Janis sat there, still buckled into her seat. But of course she wasn't actually sitting; she was lying on her side, on an air bag. A side air bag. Her eyes were closed and she was making little groaning sounds.

"Janis! Janis! Are you okay? Are you okay? Oh, god..." Carole's voice was hoarse and shaky.

"Not fucking okay...went into the ditch...you fucking cut me...off...oh, shit," Janis muttered, and groaned again, eyes still closed.

"Look at me! Can you move? Can you turn your head? Please open your eyes!" Carole was almost crying. Bending from the waist, she let herself down farther into the interior, anchored by her lower torso and legs outside the car. Distractedly, she heard a motorcycle pull up outside, then the squawk of the walkie-talkie and Abby's voice, but from her position she couldn't see anyone.

"Carole! Is Janis hurt?"

"I don't know! Call an ambulance! Janis!" Carole reached down to touch her shoulder. "Please look at me!"

Slowly Janis turned her head and opened her eyes to look at Carole. "See...can move my head," she croaked. At the sight of the familiar blue eyes, Carole's filled up, and a couple of drops fell down onto Janis's shoulder.

"Can you move your arms and legs?"

Janis moved the arm closest to Carole. "Other stuck..." Her left arm was imprisoned between her body and the air bag she was lying on. But she wiggled both hands and feet.

"Does anything hurt?" Carole managed to unbuckle the seat belt. Gravity pulled it down to fall on the air bag.

Janis didn't answer right away, as if she were checking for aches and pains. "Not...much...'m okay. Get me out."

Janis turned her upper body toward Carole, and Carole grasped her shoulders. Janis reached up her right arm and grabbed the outside edge of the passenger seat, and together they managed to pull her up enough so that she was kneeling on the air bag. They paused to get their breath, and Janis tested her left arm. "Hurts. I think it's broken." She spoke slowly but normally.

All that gym work paid off. They were both strong women and, with some help from Carole, and from Abby waiting outside, Janis was able to climb out of the car and down. But when they were back on the ground, she collapsed on a dusty strip of grass beside the ditch, moaning a little, her face white. "Arm hurts like fuck."

Carole sat and gathered her in her arms, cradling her head

and shoulders against her chest as Janis closed her eyes and seemed to pass out.

Carole looked up at Abby. "It's all my fault. It's my fault. She could have died," she sobbed, as more tears tracked her grimy face.

Abby bent down and patted Carole's head sympathetically. "I don't know exactly what happened here, hon," she said soothingly. "We didn't see it up close, but she'll be okay. She's in shock. We've called an ambulance. We'll get her checked out." She moved away, and spoke into the walkie-talkie again. Carole heard her say, "She's okay."

By this time some of the others had gathered at the accident scene. They regarded the two women curiously, but discreetly kept their distance. Carole took no notice. Hardly knowing what she was doing, she buried her face in Janis's neck.

"Hey, it's okay," Janis whispered in her ear. "I'm okay, just tired." Her good arm came around Carole's neck, pulling her closer.

"I almost lost you."

"I'm not going anywhere." Carole could feel her smiling. She pulled away slightly, looking into Janis's face. Janis's eyes were clear.

"I'm so sorry. It's all my fault. I cut you off." Carole's eyes started tearing up again.

"Maybe. But I didn't slow down enough around that corner. When you passed me, I couldn't control the car and she went across the road, heading for the cornfield ditch. I yanked the wheel and she went for the other ditch, too fast to straighten out. She slid on her side along the ditch forever. That was scary." Janis shuddered "I bet the grass in the ditch is all flattened out."

Carole looked. Indeed it was, flat for maybe forty feet.

"Good thing about the side bag," Janis continued, rambling a little. "Sure scared the hell out of me when that exploded. Probably broke my arm. Better than my head. Is my car okay?"

"I think it's fine. The side might need a paint job. We'll get the wrecker to pull her out. I'll call them after the ambulance picks you up, then find you at the hospital."

"Good," Janis said. "I'm so tired." She pulled Carole close again and closed her eyes.

In the distance they could hear the faint wail of a siren. Abby's walkie-talkie squawked again.

"Attention, please," she called out to the women milling about. "Here comes the ambulance, so before it gets here you'd better all leave, in the opposite direction. This was just an ordinary traffic accident, right? We'll all meet at Red Emma's later."

The women dispersed quickly. As the last few were leaving, Carole heard one of them say in a shocked voice, "Carole and Janis? Are you kidding me? Those two butches? No way!"

Way.

HARD TO HATE HER

Kris Adams

The large house filled Carol with a mixture of envy and regret. Once upon a time, this would have been her house, back when she was married and had no idea her husband was a snake. She honked the horn and waited for the kids to come out, ending their twice-monthly weekend with their dad and his new wife.

After two more honks she sighed dramatically and forced herself out of the car.

Three rings on the doorbell and still no kids. Then she heard water splashing behind the house—the pool. The pool that her kids raved about and that made their visits run late. The pool that she'd never be able to afford on her own. The pool her kids were probably playing in right now, only to then fill her small car with the stink of chlorine.

Following the sound of the water, Carol trudged down the pathway leading to the backyard. The huge trees concealed the magnitude of the property only from afar; from this close, it was clear that the little money Dan sent her each month was merely a drop in his deep bucket. Carol took a cleansing breath, and then pushed forward.

"Hello?" She came around to the gate that led to the fenced-in pool. It was huge, like the yard, like the house, like the gas-guzzling behemoth that Dan drove when he had the kids. "Anyone home?"

The splash on the far, deep end of the pool startled her. A woman popped up, flipped a long mass of dirty-blonde hair, and fell back into the water like a great white shark breaching with a seal in its jaws. *Great,* Carol thought.

Eventually the woman resurfaced and slinked gracefully out of the pool. The waning sunlight glistened on her body, blonde and bronzed, and practically naked. Carol opened her mouth to announce her presence but found herself suddenly mute. To her utter dismay, she couldn't stop staring. The woman had an amazing body, and Carol was never one to pass up the chance to enjoy a thing of beauty.

"Um, hello."

Caught in mid–hair flip, the woman spun around to see Carol waving at her embarrassedly. "Oh! I didn't see you there!"

"Sorry. I honked. And then I rang the bell. I heard noises, so I thought the kids were…uh, are the kids here?"

"Dan will have them back soon, I think. Sorry he's late." The woman made a *You know how he is* face, which irritated Carol for several reasons. "I think they went for ice cream or something." Rubbing a fluffy towel over her belly, she approached Carol with a surprised yet friendly smile. "How've you been, Carol?"

"Okay, I guess." The familiarity with which the woman addressed her was a little unsettling—Carol was surprised she even remembered her name. "How have you been…Lily?"

"I've been good. Thanks." Tilting her head to one side, Lily wrung water from the twist of her long hair. "I've been so eager to get in the pool, but the water is too cold today!"

"Hm." Carol looked at her watch. "It has been deceptively warm these last couple of days."

Lily nodded. "Exactly. I should have turned the pool heater on, but—"

"I didn't mean to disturb your...swim...or anything, so I can just wait in the car."

Lily cleared her throat and looked down at her perfectly manicured toes. "Oh. Well, I mean, who knows when they'll be back." She reached out, her hand inches away from where Carol's was angrily clutching the top of the gate. "Why don't you come in?"

"Oh, I couldn't."

"Or, I mean it's kind of cold, but...you want to go for a swim?"

Carol wondered momentarily if tossing her cell phone in the pool could generate enough electricity to electrocute someone to death.

"It'll warm up soon. It's very relaxing!"

I know how relaxing a pool can be, Carol thought angrily. What she said, though, was, "No, but thanks."

"If you're sure." Lily smiled as she laid her hand on the gate, where it just brushed against Carol's. Carol looked down at her own hand, and wondered why it suddenly felt so warm and tingly.

"Carol? Are you okay?"

"What?" Carol didn't think anything was registering on her face, but Lily was looking at her strangely. *What the hell is wrong with me, she thought.*

"Would you like to come in for some tea?"

Carol imagined her best girlfriends growling and hissing at this moment, but she couldn't think of any good reason not to go in, save the obvious, that she, officially, hated this woman. "Well, I guess I could—"

"Mom!" Carol jumped back like she'd been caught doing something naughty. Her two kids, ice cream cone in one hand, overnight bag in the other, stared at her perplexedly from the driveway. Her twelve-year-old son Glen asked, "What are you *doing*?"

"Your mom and I were just having a chat," Lily answered confidently. "Isn't that great?"

Dani, Carol's ten-year-old daughter, rolled her eyes. "Whatever. Can we go?"

"Yes!" Carol looked between her kids and Lily and the pool and for the life of her couldn't think of what to say. "So, um, have a nice swim, Lily."

"You, too! I mean, uh, have a nice...oh...whatever. Bye, kids!" The children made noncommittal noises and waved without looking back. Lily looked down, like she wasn't really expecting a proper good-bye, but it would have been nice to get one anyway. Carol felt a strange twinge in her gut.

"Well, bye, Lily." She walked a few steps away before she heard a soft, "It was nice talking to you," from behind her.

Carol's local grocery was okay, but sometimes she liked to visit the gigantic, super-green food emporium that just happened to be in her ex's neighborhood. She walked around, looking at everything that was supposed to be so healthy, and yet was so expensive. After buying a pack of gum, she proceeded to pick up her children. Two hours early.

She rang only twice, then perked her ears toward the backyard. It had been hot, so it was a likely assumption that anyone home might be taking a dip. When she heard splashing, she assumed the whole family was in their backyard, enjoying the late spring evening. It was an easy guess to make, so she didn't hesitate to walk to the backyard gate and take a good look.

She was right in guessing that the great white would be there, terrorizing the pool with its predatory breaches. What Carol hadn't guessed was that it would be doing it in the nude.

It took Carol a second—at first she thought Lily was just wearing a very small, flesh-colored bikini. Then Lily turned to float on her back, arms and legs spread gracefully on the water, wide and glorious, and Carol could see very plainly that there was no bikini, no embarrassment, no shame.

"Shit!" Carol tried to run away, but she somehow got tangled in the low-hanging vines of the killer trees surrounding the house. And then a watering jug's handle somehow ended up on her foot. Carol's mortification was complete. "S-sorry!" she screamed over her back and with eyes squeezed shut. "I didn't know you were here...alone...and with no...sorry!"

"Carol, hi!" Carol squealed again when she felt Lily right behind her, tapping her shoulder. "Oh, dear! You okay?"

"No, I...got...caught...your trellis or whatever."

"Here." Lily, now in a short white terry-cloth robe tied loosely at the waist, had slipped out of the gate and was helping to remove a wayward stick from Carol's hair. "I think you're free now!"

"Yeah, thanks." Carol turned around, opened her eyes and unintentionally caught a glimpse of cleavage and flat belly exposed by the gaping robe. "I'm sorry, I know I'm early. I thought—again—that the kids were here and...I think I'll just go."

"But why? By the time you get home, you'll just have to drive back to pick them up, right?" Before Carol could answer, Lily was nodding and pulling her by the elbow. "Come on in.

They won't be back for a while, and...uh...you can keep me company." She closed the gate behind them and sauntered over to the deck table and chairs, which looked more expensive than Carol's indoor dining room set. "Have a seat. Relax."

"No. Thanks. I shouldn't have interrupted, I can just—"

"Please sit, Carol." Lily wrapped her robe around her a little tighter and then pointed to the pool. "Why don't you take a dip? It's so hot."

"Yeah, it is hot." Carol nervously rubbed her hand through her hair. "No, but thanks."

"Are you sure? You can borrow a suit." Lily smiled innocently, like she had no concept of dress sizes and square pegs in round holes.

"No, I'm fine. You, um, go ahead. I didn't mean to...disturb you." Carol's eyes helplessly darted to the glass of wine already on the table. Lily looked too, then smiled and headed toward the house.

"I'll get you a glass."

It was definitely weird, sitting by the pool, drinking wine and talking about the weather with the woman who stole your husband. And yet, as much as Carol hated to admit it, Lily was... not so terrible. They'd only been in the same space a handful of times, at the kids' band concerts and dance recitals. Lily had always been lovely to her and the kids, which pissed Carol off. It would be so much easier to hate her if she was the conniving, backstabbing hussy that Carol always imagined.

"Penny for your thoughts?"

"What? Oh. Um, do you swim...naked...all the time?"

Lily giggled and lay back in her deck chair. "Oh, I don't walk around the house naked when the kids are here, if that's what you're asking."

"I know you wouldn't—I mean, I hope not." Carol shook

her head at herself. This was not the knock-down, drag-out fight she assumed she'd be having if she was ever alone with Lily.

"I mean, the yard is soooo big, and with all the foliage and stuff, none of the neighbors can see, I promise."

"I believe you," chuckled Carol, now on her second glass of wine.

"Are you sure you don't want to borrow something to swim in? The water's great tonight, perfect temperature." Lily sat up and reached over to pat Carol's arm encouragingly. "Come on."

"No, but...don't let me stop you." It was the opposite of what Carol was thinking, but then Lily shrugged and started for the pool, and Carol suddenly didn't know what to think.

It was hard to tell if the graceful way Lily discarded her robe was for show or not. Carol tipped her glass to her face and looked over the rim as Lily descended into the pool. The lights inside and above the pool reflected on the ripples in the water— it was a perfectly marvelous nighttime sight, and Carol knew right away that she shouldn't have had that second glass.

"So, um...how's this book?" Carol reached over to Lily's chair and picked up the must-read hardback of the year. "Is it as good as the one before it?"

"I haven't read the first one yet. They only had it in paperback at the store, and I hate reading paperbacks." Carol felt perversely satisfied at Lily's snobbery, at least she did until Lily paused, leaning on her hands on the side of the pool, and added, "Hard-back books feel more like real books, like those thick, dusty ones that your grandparents gave you, you know? And the text is bigger, easier to read. And paperbacks are so easy to misplace. And you can't donate them to the library when you're finished—"

"Right, right." Carol wanted to pout.

"Have you read this one yet?"

"No, but I'm like number sixty-five on the wait list at the library. I should get it some time around 2011!"

Lily's brow wrinkled in the middle. "Why don't you just buy it?"

Carol refused to blush, even though her face craved the blood. "Well, it gets expensive to buy books all the time, and…they get new books at my library really quickly."

"Oh." Lily smoothed her long hair out of her eyes. "That's actually a good idea."

Right, Carol thought, *like you have to economize*. When she thought of the lame settlement she'd agreed to three years ago, when she'd wanted to be independent, and before Dan's huge promotion, it made her livid. It was only with the "extra" cash he sometimes sent her that she could afford little luxuries, usually for the kids.

"Did, um, Dan say when they'd be back, exactly?"

Lily frowned. "Um, no. Sorry." She swam away still frowning a little. Carol figured no one had ever rejected her company before. *Good.*

"I should probably just go."

"Sure," Lily murmured as she floated, on her back, her eyes up at the night sky. Carol kept her eyes on the house.

"Well, I guess I *could*—" Carol was thankful she didn't have to finish her admission. The sound of the triple garage doors opening quieted Carol and sent Lily swimming frantically over to the side of the pool.

"Shoot! Can you hand me my robe?"

"Yeah!" Carol picked it up from where Lily had casually discarded it and rushed to the pool where Lily waited, only her head above water, her face bright pink. When she got there, Lily quickly emerged, eyes big and bright and embarrassed, long hair just barely covering bouncing breasts and hard—

"Ooph!"

"S-sorry!" In the haste to get Lily covered before the kids saw her and hit puberty right then and there, both women pushed forward and ended up knocking foreheads a little. They giggled as they rushed to get the now damp robe open. Carol finally had to hold it while Lily slipped her arms in, her wet hair brushing Carol's nose and dripping down the front of her blouse. *She doesn't smell like chlorine at all,* Carol thought miserably.

"That was close!" Lily turned around, and they were suddenly standing so close that Carol had to step back.

"I should go. I'll just...could you tell them that I'll be in the car?"

"Sure." Lily tied the robe tight around her waist, which was pointless. It was short and white and clung to her wet skin. Carol pointed toward where she thought she'd parked her car—she really couldn't remember anything at that moment.

"I'll just...yeah."

Lily smiled and waved a little sadly. "See you around?"

"See you." Carol turned and practically ran to her car.

The next Friday, Carol stopped Dani just as she was leaving the car. "Here, give this book to your step—to Lily."

"Why?"

"She asked to borrow it," Carol lied. She watched the children rush down the side pathway to the backyard, to the pool, where their stepmother was probably waiting to do tricks for them. "Shoot."

"Mom, we're home!"

Carol trudged downstairs as she wondered why the kids were bothering to announce themselves. She almost dropped the water glass in her hand when she saw Lily right outside the front door.

"Hi," she squeaked, waving at Carol, who wanted to cringe in her cutoffs and stained sweatshirt.

"Hello, Lily." The front door was swinging wide open, letting the cool night air rush in, but Carol wasn't about to step forward to close it. "Thanks for bringing the kids home."

"I had to make a stop at the mall, that's why we're a little late."

"No problem." Carol squirmed, biting her bottom lip.

"And, um..." Lily's smile turned from saccharine to genuine. "Thanks for lending me the book. I'll get it back to you as soon as I can."

"Take your time. I hope you like it."

"Oh, I know I will!" Lily cleared her throat and rolled her eyes. "God, I sound like a cheerleader." Carol nodded; she could absolutely picture that. "Sorry, I'm just..." She shook her head. "Well, since I'm here...here." Lily stuck her hand into the house, holding out an unsealed business envelope. The check.

"Thanks." Carol took it and held it down at her side like it had a large red *D*-minus scratched across it. Getting handed her child support and alimony from Lily just felt wrong, somehow. "Well, enjoy the book."

Lily's smile withered just a little. "I will. Thanks again. Bye." Carol watched her jog back to her car before closing the door and looking at the envelope. It was already stamped and addressed in Dan's handwriting, but it had obviously been reopened. And it was thicker than usual.

"Extra! Must be something for the kids," Carol sighed as she ripped open the envelope, which held the check and another, wallet-sized envelope—a gift card from the local megabookstore chain. "What's this?"

"Are you and Lily, like, friends now?" Glen asked absent-mindedly as he strolled into the room.

"Do you have a book report coming up or something?"

Glen shrugged and nodded toward the gift card. "Did you read the note inside?"

"No." She flipped open the holder to the neatly written note. *Reading is Fundamental.* It didn't look at all like Dan's chicken scratch. "Did your father give you this?"

"Please. When have you ever seen Dad in a bookstore?" Heading for the kitchen, the boy laughed and shouted over his shoulder, "I told her to write *Library books suck* instead, but she wouldn't go for it!"

"No way." Carol's eyes went wide when she saw the amount of the card—three hundred dollars—the exact amount of all the previous "gifts" from her ex-husband. "Oh, my god," Carol whispered to herself, "it was her all along."

Carol could always count on her friend Angela for cheering up, retail therapy, and Dan-bashing. In the past she reveled in her friend's creative abuses of her ex-husband, but lately she couldn't bother to hate him with as much ferocity. She was just about to explain as much when Angela stopped them in the middle of the mall food court.

"What?"

"Look at what's coming this way." Carol followed Angela's line of vision. Lily was walking toward them wearing cutoffs and an old tee, yet still looking every bit the drop-dead gorgeous home wrecker.

"Hi, Carol." Lily's smile was cautiously friendly. She extended her hand to Angela, who just smirked at it. "I'm Lily."

"Oh, I know who—"

"This is Lily—Dan's wife—the kids' stepmother," Carol stammered. "This is my friend Angela." She gave her friend a pleading look, hoping to god that she wouldn't make a scene.

"Doing some shopping, Lily?"

"Oh, you know. Just walking around." Lily finally took back her hand.

"Yeeeaaah. Well, Angela, are you about ready to—"

"How is Dan?" Angela asked with mock interest. "Still into those gigantic monster SUVs?"

Carol cleared her throat, but Lily laughed it off. "Afraid so. I think they're awful, too."

Angela rolled her eyes. "Really."

"Yeah, but he loves his toys."

"Apparently."

Carol clawed at her friend's sleeve. "Angie?"

"So, Lily, what do you drive, if you don't mind my asking?"

Lily pulled her hair behind her ears. "I have a Jag."

"Of course you—"

"But most days I drive my Prius."

Angela folded her arms across her chest. "Well, aren't you the green one? You've got your secondhand husband and your hybrid car—there's no stopping you, is there?"

Carol nearly choked on her own tongue. "You know what, we should—"

"No, I was just...nice to...yeah." Lily forced a tense smile and quickly walked away. Carol could barely look Angela in the eye.

"I can't believe you were so nice to her!"

"Let's just go," Carol mumbled to her feet. She couldn't believe a lot of things lately.

It was dusk, and Carol wondered what the setting sun's rays would look like reflected on the pool—or anything in it. She didn't bother ringing the bell, just went directly to the backyard.

When she got there, Lily was staring at the sky, arms over her head, hands resting on her neck. She was a vision.

"Lily?"

"We weren't expecting you until later. I'm afraid I'm the only one here."

"Good," Carol admitted, her mouth dry. "I came to see you."

"Hm." Lily finally looked at her husband's first wife. "Why?"

"I wanted to apologize for Angela. In the mall? She can be... blunt."

"She was just being honest." Her shoulders fell, and she suddenly looked very vulnerable in her silk caftan. "She has every right to hate me, just like you do."

"I don't hate you." It was bizarre realizing that she actually did not hate this woman. She really intensely did not hate her. It was a scary thought...a little exciting, too. "Not that I don't have reason to! I mean, you did...well..."

"Ruin your marriage." Carol wondered if great white sharks were capable of expressing remorse. "Dan cheated on you with me...and then he married me." Lily looked down at the ring on her finger. "So you hate me."

Carol opened the gate and slipped inside the yard. "Can you blame me? Not that I want Dan back. I'm over him, completely." They both seemed to breathe a little easier. It never occurred to Carol that Lily might be nervous about that. "But, yes. What you did wasn't...a nice thing to do to someone."

"You're right. I used to...I still do...sort of...feel bad about that." All Carol could think was *Wow*. "But I don't know how to, or if I even should...say I'm...um...sorry."

"Why are you telling me this now?"

Lily sank down into a wicker loveseat and stared off into space until Carol sat down beside her. "I've always wanted to say this to you, but I wasn't sure how. And we've never really had the chance to talk before, and...you're so nice." Carol smiled. "No, I mean it. You've never been rude to me or anything. I couldn't blame you if you resented me." Lily reached out tentatively, like she was afraid of burning her hand, before gently grasping Carol's wrist. "I'm sorry that I hurt you, Carol. You didn't deserve that. It makes me sad to think that your life changed drastically because of me."

Carol watched Lily's fingers rubbing her skin, which suddenly felt hot. "You feel sorry for me."

"No, that's not what I—"

"That explains the extra money. I thought it was from Dan. I didn't know it was guilt money to ease your conscience."

"I guess I deserve that. I'm sorry." Lily started to pull her hand away, but Carol reflexively grabbed and held it tight before she lost the chance.

Lily looked away, across the huge yard into the trees shielding them from the world. "Maybe it was guilt money, but I didn't intend it that way. I know what your settlement was, and it should have been more. Dan can be, well, frugal." Hearing Carol giggling, Lily turned back and smiled shyly. "I guess you already knew that!"

"Yeah." Lily turned her hand so their palms touched, fingers entwined. It felt very strange, intimate, and delicious. "Thanks. The extra money definitely helped."

Lily looked up at Carol with huge eyes. "You want to go swimming with me?"

"I don't have anything to wear," Carol answered, though she'd already made up her mind.

"That's okay." Lily stood, still holding Carol's hand. "No one's watching but me."

The robe Lily gave her barely covered her naked ass. Carol

tried to hold it closed as she walked out of the house and accepted a wineglass from Lily.

"This robe is too small for me."

"You'll only have it on a minute," Lily answered as she led Carol to the heated pool.

"It's been ages since I've been swimming," Carol murmured, nervously.

"What about skinny-dipping?"

"N-never."

Lily took Carol's glass from her. "Then it's time you start."

"Yes." After a deep breath, Carol shook the small white robe off and walked down the steps into the pool. Even with eyes closed she could tell Lily was watching her. She dove under to hide her smile, then surfaced to float on her back.

It was quiet for a while. Carol swam and floated lazily, enjoying the warm water on her face and chest, and the way it lapped between her legs. It felt like heaven, both in spite of and because of the eyes following her. After a while she called out, "Aren't you coming in?"

"Just admiring the view." When Carol suddenly looked up, Lily was blushingly finishing her glass of wine. Carol waded into waist-deep water.

"I think that was my glass."

Putting both glasses down, Lily licked her lips and murmured, "I guess I have a history of wanting things that belong to you."

Carol's skin went to gooseflesh. "Is that so?" Lily pulled off the caftan, tossed it aside and walked naked into the pool, inches from where Carol was shivering in the warm water.

"That's so." Before Carol could speak, Lily grabbed her hands and sputtered, "I'm sorry for everything, Carol. I hope you can forgive me one day. I just...want to be a good person."

"You are a good person."

"So are you." It must have been the water that brought them together. Carol didn't notice either of them moving forward, but somehow they ended up in each other's arms, hugging close, breathing on necks and in wet hair, their breasts pressing closer with each breath. Carol could feel both their hearts racing.

"You're making it very hard to hate you, Lily."

"Good." Pulling away to look Carol in the eye, Lily placed both hands on Carol's face, smoothing the hair back behind Carol's ears. "You make it real easy to like you." She traced Carol's cheekbones, her nose, and then her open mouth. "Like you a lot."

"Oh." It was the strangest thing that had ever happened to Carol, being naked in the arms of the woman who, she used to think, ruined her life. Part of her wanted to thank Dan—if he hadn't been such a bastard, she'd never have been here, about to kiss the most beautiful shark in the ocean.

It was brief at first, just a small press of lips, until Lily asked, "Is this okay?" and Carol answered with a deeper kiss.

Just as she felt her knees start to wobble, Carol pulled back and whispered, "I like you, too. In case you were wondering." Lily made a high pitched squeak in her throat and dove back in for more.

The swimming pool was calm, and empty. Upstairs, Carol kicked a tangled silk sheet off the bed and watched breathlessly as Lily licked a mixture of sweat and other secretions from the inside of her thigh. "Taking the day off from work was the best idea we've had in months."

"Definitely." Lily kissed a line from thigh to mons to navel before looking up with hopeful eyes. "Carol?"

"Honey."

"I've been thinking. Wouldn't the ultimate revenge against

a cheating ex-husband be to steal away the woman he cheated with in the first place...and then move in with her?" she added quickly.

Carol's brow wrinkled. "This isn't about revenge. It's about us...right?"

"You didn't answer the question, baby."

"Are you serious?"

"Look, if you don't want to, just say so."

"Lily." Carol's voice dropped to a near whisper. "You would leave Dan for me?"

"Yes, I would."

Carol's heart began to race, faster than it did earlier, when they'd torn each other's clothes to shreds to get inside each other. "But...your house."

"Do you really think that matters to me?"

After months of spending nearly all their free time together, publicly as new friends, privately as lovers, Carol thought she knew almost everything about this woman. She smiled and pulled Lily up into a kiss. "Okay. Come home with me. To stay."

Lily smiled and laid her head on Carol's chest. They stroked each other's bodies quietly for a while before she cleared her throat and stated, "By the way...this is my house. I bought it before I married Dan. I had a really lucrative dot-com in the nineties and got out before the bubble burst. Then I invested wisely and...well, I'm not filthy rich, but...I'm kind of well off. All on my own."

Carol shook her head. It was nothing but wonderful surprises with Lily from the start. "Figures. So why didn't you ever tell me? Were you worried I'd only want you for your money?"

"Money's important," Lily sighed. "Money makes people do stupid things. Like marry the wrong person."

Carol hesitated. "So what now?"

"It's up to you. Just know that...I can help take care of you
and the kids. That's not something you'd ever have to worry
about again."

Carol could feel her throat start to tighten; she needed to get
everything out before she couldn't talk. "Why would you do
that?"

"Because you were kind to me when you didn't have to be.
Because you accepted my friendship when you didn't have to.
And...because I'm in love with you."

Carol waited to say it back until she was back in the pool,
watching Lily make graceful breaches for no one's eyes but hers.
It was the place where they first kissed, made love, met, and Carol
blurted the three words out like she'd explode if she didn't. Lily
kissed her and floated back into the deep end, smiling proudly
like she knew the truth all along.

QUEENS UP

Andrea Dale

It was my daddy who taught me to play poker.

He was a good father as fathers go, I suppose, especially considering my mother died when I was four and he had his hands full raising me. He was also a very good teacher, and I was hustling the ranch hands before some of them realized the ragged moppet who dogged their heels was not, in fact, of the male persuasion. Took them a right long while, too, considering how I'd been so modest about peeing in front of 'em.

I tended toward wearing men's clothes even as I grew older, because it was much easier roping cattle in breeches than a skirt, and skirts were just nuisances anyway, not to mention stockings and petticoats, and besides, there was no one around to properly lace me into a corset.

Even my childhood playmate Margaret Compton didn't know when we were children. Which is why when we grew older things grew a mite complicated, because I had a crush on her.

In the end, though, it worked out fine, because sweet Margaret

Compton wasn't about to go getting any crushes on men, either, and when she found out my secret, well, we then had a delicious secret to share, just between us two.

But I was talking about my daddy.

For all he was a good man at heart, the problem was simple. There was one other thing that he was good at, and that was drinking. So, for all his good teaching of the cards, my father wasn't a very good poker *player* at all.

Which is how he came to lose our family's ranch to one Mister Samuel Owens.

By the time this happened, I'd been running the ranch for years, not that anyone outside knew that. Wasn't proper for a woman to be making such decisions—what did a pretty thing know about cattle and budgets and weather patterns and ordering men around? So my daddy was the figurehead, the one who went to the bank and the auctions (on mornings after I'd hidden his bottles so his head would be clear). Me, I balanced the books and wrote up orders for supplies and, yes, bossed the men around, but by that time they knew I was capable and cared enough about the ranch to keep our secret safe.

God took pity on me the next morning when Samuel came out to the ranch to take a good, long look at his new ownings (not that I knew the reason for his visit as yet).

I wasn't riding out on the back forty or forking hay off a wagon that day. Instead, I was inside catching up on some business correspondence for my daddy to sign when he woke up from last night's binge, and Margaret had time to run in and let me know company was approaching.

I'd have to play hostess while someone roused Daddy and stuck his head under the pump to shock some soberness into him.

Margaret was more versed in the intricacies of women's

clothing than I, so she rushed about gathering skirts and boots with tiny buttons and whatever else I'd need to shoehorn myself into.

At that point in our relationship, we had to keep things pretty quiet, so Margaret slept in the servants' quarters and our trysts were rare, stolen moments. Her own daddy had died coming up on two years ago, and I'd promised him that I'd take care of Margaret as if she were one of my own. And she was my own—she had my heart, and I hers. By outside appearances, she was our maid and cook, and when the occasional hand took a fancy to courting her, she smiled and gently eased his attentions aside.

My point being, when I looked up from shucking my shirt and trousers, I shouldn't have been surprised by the look in her eyes.

Hunger. Need. Lust.

The same sensations flared through me, ignited a fire in my belly—and below.

Aware of my own foolishness, I still couldn't help but step toward her, take her face in my hands, and kiss her.

Every time I kissed her was heaven, but it had been far too long since we'd been able to be together, and so the sweet heat of her mouth was a desperate homecoming. I wanted to devour her, be devoured by her. Her tongue danced with mine, and all I could think of was how that tongue felt in the hollow of my shoulder, on the hard peak of my breast, at the juncture between my thighs.

I moaned, and she answered. I wound my fingers into the honey-colored upsweep of her soft hair and kissed her as if I were making love to her. Right now this was the only moment I had, and if I didn't have time to strip her and lay her down beside me and love her properly, I could at least do this.

But it couldn't be that way, and it couldn't go on forever.

Her whimper as I pulled away almost drove me to my knees, because her desperation and desire mirrored my own. I was hot and wet and quivering on the edge, and all I'd done was kiss her.

If her hands hadn't been full of my dress and petticoats and stockings—if she'd stroked between my legs—I would have known the oblivion I craved.

No time. I kissed her on the tip of her pert nose, and whispered my love and apologies. One reason I love her is that she understands the tightrope I must walk.

It was excruciating to feel her hands on me and have them putting clothes on me, not stripping them off. Every tug that tightened my corset lacings was like a step closer to the gallows. How I ached to be naked in her arms, breasts pressed to breasts, fingertips chasing over skin and raising gooseflesh and desire.

Later. I promised us both that.

My father was being fetched, and Samuel Owens awaited me in the parlor.

"Why, Miss Josephine, you are quite a sight today," Samuel said, rising with his hat in his hand to greet me. Oh, he might have said the right words, acted all solicitous and proper, but his eyes revealed his true thoughts. His gaze raked over me, greedy and lascivious, a disgusting parody of the way Margaret had stared in awe at my figure just a few moments ago.

Oily, I thought. Oily Owens, that's what they called him behind his back, and I could see why.

"And a good day to you, Mr. Owens," I said, my smile as sweet as I could manage, and him no wiser for it. "What brings you out here this fine day?"

His eyebrows shot up. "Your daddy didn't tell you?"

Now I felt like *I'd* been sitting under the water pump. *Oh, Daddy, what have you done?*

"I haven't spoken to my father yet today," I said. "He's been..."

I couldn't say *indisposed,* because I guessed Samuel Owens had been witness to my daddy's drinking the night before.

"...occupied," I finished.

Samuel wasn't a good enough actor to suppress a snort of derision, although he seemed to catch himself enough to bite back whatever it was his first instinct to say.

"Well, now, I hope he's not too occupied to see me," he said. "We have some business to attend to, your father and I. You might want to fetch him, Miss Josephine, and hear what needs to be said, as it involves you."

At first I couldn't imagine what business Samuel might have with my father (since I knew firsthand what-all business was to be had regarding the workings of the ranch), much less how it could involve me.

But I'm not stupid, and a sick gnawing started in my chest that had nothing to do with the tightness of my corset.

When Daddy wouldn't meet my eye as we sat down at the kitchen table, I knew something was very, very wrong. Much worse than just another dreadful night at the card table.

"Jo—Josephine," Daddy said. "I had a run of bad luck with the cards last night..."

And I knew, with head-spinning certainty, what he'd done.

I would not—would *not*—faint like a simpering girl. No matter how hard it was to draw in a full breath in this damnable contraption.

"Now, Miss Josephine," Samuel broke in, "I'm not a hard-hearted man. I know we can come to an equitable agreement that keeps your family's ranch intact."

I was certain his heart was as hard as another part of him, given the way he couldn't keep his eyes off the swell of my breasts, but I held my tongue.

It came as no real surprise that the ranch wasn't really what Samuel had sought to win in that game. What my daddy had thoughtlessly tossed into the pot, believing his hand was the unbeatable one, was me. *My* hand—in marriage.

Well, of course I gathered what dignity I could and politely told Mr. Samuel Owens that we appreciated his offer greatly, but that my hand was not available at this time, and wasn't there some other way we could resolve this issue to our mutual satisfaction?

The fact was simple: "No, there is not."

He said the words quietly, outwardly calm, but the way his face flushed and his hat shook in his hands made it clear he was reining in his anger.

Seeing as we were all in the middle of calving season, he said, he'd give me two weeks to think over his offer. At the end of those two weeks, if my answer was the same as it was now, then we would have three days to remove ourselves and our belongings from the premises, or Samuel would see to it that the sheriff did so.

Then he stood, jammed his hat back on his head, and walked out of the house, his footsteps slamming down on the floorboards of the porch as if he were marking the house as his own with his boot heels.

We did not have the money to buy the ranch back from Samuel.

We did not have anywhere to go, or any real means of income, without the ranch.

Oh, we could go work on someone else's ranch—if I had to scrub floors, I was perfectly capable of doing so—but my father's health wouldn't allow for riding the range or baling hay, and I couldn't support him on a maid's salary.

There was whoring, of course, but if I was going to do that, I might as well marry Samuel and keep the ranch in the family.

My father, bless him, never said a word about that, never spoke once about that arrangement being the only thing that could save us. I saw it in his eyes, when he thought I wasn't looking. But he never said it aloud, and I loved him for that.

We were four days from our deadline, with no miracle in sight, and Margaret had been quietly packing up my mother's bone china when my father wasn't around (I had already been through her jewelry, estimating how much I could get for it and how long we could live on that money), when a chance—just a fleeting chance—presented itself.

One of the hands happened to mention the rumor of a poker game in Haldern City: A high-stakes game, with men coming from all over the territory to participate.

The type of game Samuel Owens wouldn't be able to pass up.

My plan was plumb crazy. I don't deny that for one second. Given what was at stake, though, crazy was all we had left.

I took a loan out against the ranch. Samuel had the deed in his hands, but hadn't told the bank that yet, and the banker was my mother's cousin once removed.

If I lost the game, I'd no doubt be seeing the next few years from the inside of a jail cell, but I had no choice.

My breasts were fortunately small; bound properly, they wouldn't be obvious. But Margaret still fretted, and I'd be lying if I said I didn't share her worries. Passing myself off as a boy when I was ten years old was different than trying it at twenty, even with a hat low over my brow and a fake mustache that in daylight looked like the runt of the litter had chosen my lip to expire on.

The only likely person to recognize me would be Samuel,

who didn't know me in anything but flounces and bows.

The hardest part was my hair. Margaret wept as she sliced the scissors through it and the long black locks littered the floor. I hadn't thought I'd care, but the sight of my shorn head in the mirror was disturbing, unreal.

How I'd explain it away after the game was something I just didn't have time to concern myself with.

I was more worried that my father would want to go to Haldern City himself, but the loss of the ranch had broken his spirit. He had nothing left to gamble away.

The thing with plans is sometimes you get so caught up in them that you don't realize someone else is making plans, too.

My sweet, cunning Margaret intended to make sure no one suspected my name wasn't Joseph.

I'd been lying for so long to keep the ranch running that it came easily to me. Still, one gentleman kept asking, "Now, what parts did you say you were come from?"

I'd mentioned a city far enough away that none of them knew it well, but I still couldn't slip up on any details. Another muttered, "Awfully skinny looking fellow," to his acquaintance.

I knew my face was too smooth. I knew my voice hovered on the high side of tenor.

If I was found out, there was no telling what they'd do. All I knew was that I'd be in a world of hurt—if I made it out of there at all—and the ranch would be lost forever.

To say I was tense during the first hand was an understatement, which is why, even with the decent cards I had, I bowed out early. I needed to focus, to concentrate, and to gauge my opponents. My father had given me a few tips about Samuel (none of which I figured I could actually count on), but most of the men were unknown to me. Two more I knew from town, but not well enough to judge them now.

I could do this. All I had to do was read my cards, read my opponents, not get greedy. Focus on Samuel, push him until he had no choice but to ante up more than he ever planned to.

"Why, Joseph, there you are!"

I knew that voice. But it couldn't be…

Tarted up with rouge and paint, her curves cinched into a tiny corset, her breasts nearly spilling out over the low-cut ruffles, Margaret was near to unrecognizable to me. She'd dyed her hair a shocking red, and the beauty spot on her cheek looked as though she'd had it since she was a squalling babe.

I stole a quick glance at Samuel, frantically trying to recall if he'd ever met her and, if he had, would he be likely to remember her face.

But he was as mesmerized as the rest of them.

The rest of *us*, I should say, because I could barely keep my eyes off of her. She was beautiful in her gaudiness, no more beautiful than she always was to me, but in a different way now.

Her fearlessness and ingenuity had a lot to do with that.

The man who kept asking where I was from—Ed was his name—actually stood and touched his forehead. "Greetings, ma'am," he said, with that touch of irony all men have when greeting saloon girls, "and who might you be?"

Her laugh tinkled musically. "Why, I'm Joseph's good luck charm, or so he says. He never plays a game without me." She leaned forward, just a little, and the men all leaned forward, just a little, hoping for a glimpse of more secret flesh. "Now, if my presence is bothering you-all, I'd be happy to wait outside."

They swallowed, they twitched, they considered. It wasn't as if we didn't have other such girls in the room, freshening our drinks, singing a song or two. There was always the chance, though, that Margaret and I could have some sort of cheating scam set up.

Samuel, of all people, spoke first. "I say let her stay," he said. "She'll no doubt distract poor Joseph here more than any of us, and that's money in our pockets!"

The others whooped and agreed. They whooped even louder when Margaret bent over me and angled for a kiss, with which I was more than happy to oblige her.

She made my head spin and my skin shiver, and for a moment she was the entirety of my world. It was only the knowledge that I had to win back the ranch so that I could give her a home, a home with me, that pulled me back to the stink and sweat and clamor of the room.

Because they expected me to, I slapped her bottom lightly and told her to get me a whiskey. With a saucy grin, she asked if any of the other gentlemen needed a refilling of their refreshments, which caused the other girls to scowl when several of my opponents took Margaret up on her offer.

Ed dealt the next hand. It was hell focusing on the cards and not on Margaret's fine bottom. Thankfully I wasn't the only one who was distracted.

I felt a little bit more confident with this hand. I was getting to know the other players, and thanks to Margaret, I wasn't as worried at being found out.

Cards were examined. Odds were considered. Bets were made.

Margaret came back and distributed drinks. I took a cautious sip of mine—it would be too obvious if I completely ignored it. Oh, smart girl! She'd watered it down.

To solidify our relationship, and to the hoots and comments of the men, she settled down on my knee.

She smelled sweet—some sort of lavender powder she'd

dusted on—and I knew she tasted even sweeter. And it'd been too long since I'd tasted that honeyed sweetness.

If I'd had male parts, I'd've been drilling through her petticoats right about then.

My thighs were sweaty and itchy in my woolen trousers, but my pearl was slick and throbbing. I couldn't resist letting my hand slide up the boning along Margaret's waist to rest on the curve of her breast. Beneath the ruffles, I knew I could find her sensitive peak. There was so much temptation to lose myself in her...but we both had to deny ourselves pleasure, and to struggle with arousal and desire.

No matter what the outcome of the game would be, I whispered her a promise: Tonight. Tonight would be ours.

My daddy always said that playing poker was a right bit more interesting than the telling of it afterward. If the game had gone badly, I wouldn't be relating this tale.

Suffice to say I got Samuel Owens where I wanted him: out of money, out of sense, and full of desperate pride. He threw the deed to my family's ranch into the pot with a comment about how the ranch wasn't as important to him as the prize he'd still get to keep. Margaret froze on my lap, but I kept my mind on the cards.

Even if I lost tonight, Samuel would never have me. It was as simple as that.

My hand wasn't the best at the table, I was sure of that. But my daddy had taught me well, and maybe being a woman made it easier for me to read the men sitting around me—or made it easier for me to keep them from reading me. A woman's best weapon is her ability to keep a secret.

I lay down my cards, and took back my destiny.

Where Margaret had gotten the money to secure a room at the hotel, I'll never know. I didn't care. Giddy on success and relief, I could only follow her.

The men who watched us go were jealous, and they had every reason to be.

She snuck a flask of whiskey up to our room, and we drank it and giggled like schoolgirls. Still, though, my hands shook as I held the deed.

"I should go home," I said. "He'll want to know what transpired."

Margaret rested a cool, long-fingered hand over mine, and I knew she understood. But I went on.

"Likely as not, though, he'll have drowned his worries in that last bottle he thinks I haven't found." I turned to Margaret, sitting on the bed beside me, and took her face in my hands. "We can be back tomorrow before he wakes up, and still have tonight."

Finally, I could kiss her again, in just the way I wanted to. Not rushed, not pretending, just the two of us, and all the time in the world.

I'd been needing her so badly and for so long that the touch of her soft lips to mine was nearly enough to send me flying. Neither of us wanted tender or slow. A moment later our teeth knocked together in our shared eagerness to kiss harder, closer, *now*.

Margaret was always beautiful to me, whether in her oldest dress, sweat beading her brow as she pounded the laundry; wearing trousers to join me when I rode out to inspect the back forty; or naked and rumpled in my bed. Now, though, I have to admit a certain baseness in that I found her astonishingly alluring in the short skirt and all-but-baring corset.

I couldn't help but snake my hand beneath the ruffles, gasping with delight when I found I'd been right that her nipple truly hadn't been restrained by the corset. Instead, it had hovered, barely covered by fabric, so close to my face all night long.

Then it was her turn to gasp—and my turn to thrill all the way down through my belly—as I rolled that tender nubbin between my fingers.

No more waiting. I pulled the fabric down, exposing the curves of her breasts above the tight line of the corset, and feasted on her rosy peaks, suckling and nipping until I swore the boning in her corset was the only thing keeping her upright.

That is, until I nudged her to lie back on the bed.

I worked my way beneath her skirts with the tenacity and skill of a prospector, and what I found was worth far more than gold to me.

She was sleek and open to me, tasting of honey and rainwater and promises. My only regret was that I couldn't see her face as I kissed her most intimate parts, and slipped two fingers inside her. I could imagine it, though. And I could hear her cry out as she spasmed around me, my sweet Margaret.

It was easy enough to get my shirt off, and she had me spinning in circles to release me from the wrapped cloth that bound my breasts. Men's clothes being as simple as they were, we had the luxury of undressing me completely before she paused, just for a moment, to stare at me with all the desire and love a woman could.

I'd so missed the feel of her mouth on me, kissing me everywhere, kisses and licks and nips until my body was on fire for her. Her own need sated for now, she felt she had more time to linger, and she laughed when I told her plainly that she would drive me mad before she was done.

With no corset to hold me, I was boneless and quivering by the time she pressed a kiss against my hip bone, then brushed her hair against that same spot as she kissed me lower still.

Then there was nothing else in the world but Margaret and me.

My daddy had taught me to trust the cards and trust myself, not anything or anyone else. Still, when I'd bluffed my way through and laid down my winning hand that night, I'd felt a certain sense of destiny: two pair, queens up.

RECLAMATION

Nell Stark and Trinity Tam

V alentine strode beside me enrobed in darkness—from the liquid silk that flowed along her arms and torso to the supple leather pants molded intimately against the long stretch of her legs. She always looked good in black, a canon I embraced whenever I had the chance to dress her, as I had tonight. Black accentuated the luminescent fairness of Val's skin and the burning gold of her short-cropped hair. Black and white, a bold aesthetic and a rigid morality, both hallmarks of my lover that had stoked my attraction in the past and would test my control tonight. Valentine was dangerous, I reminded myself, even as my body sidled closer to hers, my bare arm brushing seductively against her silken sleeve.

One did not tease a vampire without the threat—or promise—of being bitten.

We hadn't slept in the same bed for almost a month, and we hadn't made love for two—not since the brutal attack that had turned her. I knew what she feared, that her thirst for my blood would get the best of her in a moment of passion—that she would lose control and take too much. She wanted to keep me safe and whole. But sleeping alone on the other side of the city in an antiseptic facility maintained by the vampires and wereshifters was not a solution. Apart, we were weak—uncertain, anxious, preoccupied. Together, we were stronger than any obstacle in our path. I believed that, and I knew that deep down, Val did too.

Tonight, I was going to remind her.

It was cliché, perhaps, dressing my vampire in black. But I couldn't resist. Valentine absorbed me like light from the visible spectrum. I knew that if she would only draw me in again, I could warm the chill from her skin and burn to ash the fear that was starving her. It's true that she fed from me, punctured my skin with her cosmetically sharpened teeth and sucked the blood from my veins to feed the parasite that thrived in hers. What she didn't believe was that I enjoyed it. I craved the warmth of her lips against me, the sharp sting of her teeth, the greedy pull of her mouth, and the hungry growl that rumbled from the depths of her when she fed. She thought herself a monster, unworthy not only of me, but of her own continuing existence. But I thought of her as an angel—beautiful, immortal, perfection poised on the precipice of falling.

Fatigue burned behind my eyes as we ascended a brief flight of stairs. I was run-down from serving as her sole source of food, while also maintaining a full course load at NYU Law. And I couldn't sleep well without her. Val wasn't getting good rest either; she'd admitted as much a few short hours ago. We were a mess. But that wouldn't change until I could convince her that the fear was harming us more than her fangs ever could. We had been inseparable, but now a chasm gaped between us. I was desperate to cross it but didn't know how. And it felt like my time was running out.

At least tonight, I had a chance. Earlier today, she had approached me with an invitation to attend a private party at Luna, one of the most exclusive clubs in the city. I had decided to buy a new dress—black, halter top, and backless—for the occasion. This was a seduction, not only of Val's body, but of her very soul. And so far, it was working. Even now, as she gently placed her hand on the small of my back to guide me through the heavy studded doors, I could feel the tautness in her muscles that belied the depth of her need.

Despite the clarity and importance of my mission, though, I was momentarily distracted by the club's architecture and décor. I felt like we had stepped into a fairytale. Luna was a tall cylinder built over a large pool of water. A glass circle the precise size of the pool was set into each floor. The circles were ringed by a broad walkway that held high tables and chairs on this floor and private booths—or so I'd heard, anyway—on the floor above.

When we found a good spot near the edge of the dancing, I slipped my arms around Val's slim waist and pressed my lips to her jaw. "Unbelievable. Un*fucking*believable."

"Yeah," Val breathed into my hair as her hands found their way to the bare skin of my back. I shivered under her touch, loving how even the lightest pressure of her fingertips against my skin could make my temperature rise, loving that the magical ambience of the club was compelling her to relax into old habits—us, the way we used to be together.

But my attention strayed momentarily as I noticed another vampire, just a few feet away, who had backed his date up against the wall and was drinking greedily from her neck. Her eyes were closed in bliss. I stifled a shudder, born of both fear and desire, at the casual intimacy of the act. On the surface, this could pass for a human party, but in reality I was very much a minority. It was an unsettling feeling, a sideways shift into an alternate universe—

And then Val slowly, deliberately walked her fingers up my naked spine.

My reaction was instinctual. I thrust my hands into her hair, pressed the length of my body against hers, and bit her chin. When she groaned quietly, I felt a surge of hope. *That's right, Val. Feel me. Feel us. Don't be afraid.*

We swayed together to the music for a while, holding each other close. I could feel the muscles in her back loosening one by one like tumblers in a lock as she relaxed in my arms. I shifted closer, and her hands slipped sensuously down my hips. I gasped in surprise as goose bumps prickled across my exposed skin at the electricity in her touch. Even now, as circumstance threatened to separate us, our bodies continued to find new ways of connecting and communicating. I started backing Val toward a vacant niche. In my mind's eye, I envisioned trapping her against the wall with my body, grasping her hair in my fingers and forcing her mouth to the throbbing pulse at my neck. I'd show her that I wasn't afraid—that I wanted her, needed her. I'd unbutton her pants and slip—

"Valentine Darrow. The new kid on the block." An unfamiliar voice shattered my daydream. The stranger stood in my peripheral vision, and I shifted in Val's embrace to get a better look. Tall, and crowned by a full head of stylishly shaggy hair, he wore a white suit and an insouciant smile that seemed oddly familiar. When he offered his hand to Val, I stepped out of the way. "Sebastian Brenner."

The name and face finally clicked in my brain—I'd read an article about him just a few weeks ago online. "You own this place," I said, hearing the faint surprise in my own words. Why was this man, by all counts one of the most up-and-coming businessmen of my generation, bothering to introduce himself to us?

He seemed bemused by my reaction. "I do indeed. And you are?"

"Alexa Newland."

He inclined his head politely but refocused his attention on Valentine right away. A flash of jealousy pierced me, churning my stomach. I was used to feeling mildly jealous when we were out—Val never failed to attract attention—but in nearly a year of being together, I had never seen a man look at her the way Sebastian Brenner was right now.

What was his game? Did he represent some attempt on the part of the vampires to seduce Val away from me? Two months ago, I would have been smug in the belief that they were going about it all wrong. Val had grown up surrounded by wealth and power, and she'd turned her back on the devil's bargain that was her family fortune. But tonight, my old insecurities clambered to the forefront. I'd grown up simply and comfortably middle-class in a small town in Wisconsin. Val's family was political and financial royalty. She claimed that she didn't want any part of that legacy, but was my presence in her life enough to turn her away from the seduction of her family name? Perhaps now that eternity defined her future, she would have far more use for the promises offered by the likes of Sebastian Brenner.

I tamped down my uncertainty and slipped into the space between them to cuddle up against Val's side, sliding one arm around her back and stroking her stomach through the silk with my other hand. I even let one finger dip into the space between two buttons to tease the skin beneath. When she tensed under my touch and inhaled in a quiet gasp, I looked up directly into Sebastian Brenner's dark gray eyes and smiled sweetly.

He raised his eyebrows, a slight grin playing around the

corners of his mouth as though getting a rise out of me had been his intent all along. I clutched Val more possessively and held the smile a moment longer than felt natural.

"Allow me to buy you both a drink."

When Val glanced at me, I nodded. I had set out tonight with the intent to prove to Valentine how important it was for us to be together. At the very least, Sebastian's attention was distracting her from brooding about how dangerous she was to me. Maybe I could use that to my advantage.

Sebastian gestured toward the stairs, and the crowds parted automatically for us at his unspoken command. When we reached the top, he bent his head to speak briefly to a woman wearing a floor-length satin gown and a fresh bite mark near one shoulder strap. The dress's deep blue color was identical to the wall paneling. Sebastian noticed Val staring at the bite, and leaned in close, his mouth almost brushing her ear.

"We vet our servers in more ways than one," he murmured.

My stomach dropped as I wondered whether Val felt desire when she looked at that woman—whether she too wanted to sink her teeth into the smooth, buttery skin of her neck. But as we moved on, she squeezed my hand. Her expression, when I caught her eye, was one of gratitude. "Love you," she mouthed, and some of my confidence trickled back.

Sebastian wove deftly through the throng of people, and we followed in his wake. As we crossed onto the glass floor, I looked down at the crowd below, writhing to the thick electronic beat. Occasionally, the bodies would separate just long enough for me to see a flash of rainbow-tinted water. Surreal. He finally paused at one of several alcoves, separated from the dance floor by a floor-to-ceiling black curtain. Flinging the fabric aside, he revealed the most luxurious booth I'd ever seen. He slid gracefully onto one of the dark blue leather benches, smoothing one hand over the chrome table in a proprietary gesture. Directly opposite the curtain, a window, cut the width of the table, looked down on the busy street below. Val indicated that I should precede her, clearly so that I could have the best view, and I kissed her lightly before sliding into place. No sooner had we settled ourselves, than the server returned, bearing a tray full of drinks.

"I took the liberty of ordering one of our specialties for you both," Sebastian said. "It's called a Waltz on the Moon."

I cradled the stem of the cocktail glass and took a small sip. A subtle blend of fruit flavors flowed over my tongue: banana liqueur, a hint of apples…and was that lychee, too? I would have to ask Val—she would know. I licked my lips, savoring the taste. "It's very good."

Turning to see Val's reaction, I froze. Her gaze was focused on my mouth, and her expression was hungry. I brought the glass to my lips again, this time closing my eyes as I sipped. Within moments, her hand was on my thigh, just above my knee. So warm. I didn't even try to halt the quiet moan that escaped me at her touch.

When I opened my eyes, smiling faintly, Val squeezed once before taking her first sip. She leaned toward Sebastian, but there was nothing flirtatious in the movement. "Tell me. Why are you giving us the VIP treatment?"

He laughed, throwing back the shot that the server had brought him with one practiced flick of his wrist. "Am I not allowed to be curious about the newest member of our little community?"

"You're no vampire," I said immediately, frowning. He had to be a shifter then, of course, and I found myself musing over the possibilities for his animal half. Something predatory, and vaguely menacing. He clearly felt himself entitled, even to other people's lovers.

The jealousy reared its head again as I realized that in certain respects, Sebastian had more in common with Val than I did. They would both live forever. They were both possessed, in a way—Val by the vampire parasite and Sebastian by the were virus. They belonged to the same club, of which I would never be a part.

"What do you become, when you shift?" I asked, wanting to know what I was up against.

He had just enough time to salute me with the empty glass before it was taken from him and replaced with a full one. "How did you guess?"

"You may not be a vampire," I said, "but you're not beneath them on the food chain, either."

He flashed his teeth at my assessment. "Technically, it *is* possible for a vampire to take blood from a shifter. But exceedingly rare." He shrugged. "The act of feeding usually triggers the change."

This new information fit with the little I already knew about weres; predators themselves, I could imagine that they didn't take well to being bitten. I looked Sebastian over again, uncertain. He carried himself like a crown prince—confident in his superiority yet effortlessly charming. He didn't seem like a loner, so it was unlikely that he was a feline. But neither did he strike me as a dependent person who wouldn't feel whole without a pack.

"So if Valentine were to bite me right now," he continued playfully, "it's likely that I would transform into a large black wolf before your very eyes, and tear out her throat. Or yours."

I shuddered at the image, and Val leaned in to kiss my neck, just behind my ear. Her lips were hot, and I shivered again out of sudden, sharp desire.

"Fortunately, you'll never have to test that theory," Val told him. The certainty behind those words and the firmness with which she'd uttered them melted away my jealousy like spring rain on snow. When she withdrew, I followed her movements, molding myself to her side.

"Never say never," Sebastian said, smirking. But the barb found no purchase this time, and I stared back at him, untroubled. He laced his fingers behind his head. "Enough about me. You're an intriguing—"

But we never got to hear exactly what it was about Val that he found so fascinating, because at that moment, a stunning South-Asian woman wearing a dark red sari ducked inside our booth and crouched next to him. She murmured something that I was unable to hear over the music, and Sebastian immediately got to his feet.

"I'm going to have to take my leave," he said as the woman stepped away. "Something has come up, and I need to attend to it immediately. I apologize." On anyone else, that might have sounded like an excuse, but he seemed genuinely regretful. "Please, feel free to stay in the booth. And your drinks are on the house."

Once he was gone, Val leaned back against the warm leather and fiddled with one of her cuff links. They were silver buttons— I had given them to her for her birthday, along with the shirt she had on right now. To the casual onlooker she seemed elegant and dangerous; I had been one myself, not so long ago. But now, I knew the depth of her intellect, her dreams and her fears; the terrible conflict between instinct and reason that was eating her alive inside. She was my soul mate. I would allow no hurdle to come between us, especially when the solution in this case was so very simple. I needed to be close to her—to be her sustenance in every possible way. She had to let go of her fear. She just had to.

"Do you want another round?" she asked, running her fingers along the hem of my dress.

I thought about Sebastian's parting words—that our drinks would be on his tab. If that was the case, I was going to indulge. "Hmm. How about scotch?"

Val's grin was wicked. "Yes. Excellent." She pulled aside the curtain just enough to flag down a server and ordered two of the finest scotches that Luna could produce—ice in a glass on the side. While we waited, I stopped her from falling back into her pensive state by pressing soft kisses to her chin, her cheeks, her jaw—showing her how much I loved her, without giving her any cause for alarm. But when the drinks arrived, I could hold myself in check no longer. I picked out the most perfect ice cube I could find, dropped it into my glass, and crawled onto Val's lap. She groaned, hands automatically going to my waist.

"You feel so, so damn good," she whispered, leaning in for a kiss.

"He wants you."

She paused inches from my mouth, clearly not expecting that response. "He wants *me*? No way. Men like him are not interested in women like me."

"You're wrong." I bypassed her lips entirely and gently took her earlobe between my teeth. When her hips bucked, a thrill of triumph ran through me. My gentle possessiveness was having exactly the effect I'd hoped.

"Doesn't...matter," Val said, her breathing harsh. "Just. Want. You."

"Oh?" I pulled back slightly to look her in the eyes. Their glazed depths revealed the extent of my power. I was going to use it. "Well, I want my scotch."

I felt the fine tremor that ran through her body at my assertive words and had to stop myself from smiling. A smile would break the mood. Val reached for my glass and swirled it once before bringing it to my mouth. I swallowed, licked my lips, and kissed her. When she sucked the scotch from my tongue, I drove my hands into her hair. The sound of her low growl made me wild with desire for her, so long denied.

When I broke the kiss she tried to complain, but I pushed two fingers into her mouth and focused on her neck. The sensation of her tongue swirling around my fingertips made me throb as I sucked hard on her pulse point. I dug in my teeth slightly, mirroring what I needed from her, and she groaned my name. It was the most beautiful sound I'd ever heard.

With one last nip at her tender skin, I eased back in her embrace until our eyes were level. Her breaths were gasps and her eyes were dark. Victory was within reach. "What do you need, Val?"

"You. Need you. So bad."

"You're coming home with me tonight." I didn't phrase it as a request.

"Yes."

The cab ride home was a struggle to remain clothed. Val pushed my dress up as high as she could without exposing me, teasing my smooth thighs with her fingertips until I was on the verge of begging her to take me right there. I retaliated by popping open each button of her shirt and pressing hot sucking kisses to the skin I revealed. She was going to have marks *everywhere*. I couldn't get enough.

We stumbled up the front steps and into the apartment, but I didn't give her any time to reflect on how it felt to finally be home again. I didn't want her to think—I wanted her to feel. To embrace who and what she was, not struggle futilely against it. Digging my fingers beneath the waistband of her pants, I tugged, pulling her into the bedroom.

"Watch," I commanded imperiously, my hands going to the

complex knot at the nape of my neck. A moment later, the dress was a black puddle at my feet. I watched the expressions move across her face like clouds running before a storm: love, desire, thirst. She resented what she had become, but I embraced it, loving the intensity of her cravings; wanting to be the only one who could satisfy her, ever. *Don't fight it, Val,* I thought as I stepped forward to divest her of her shirt. *Feel everything. Don't be afraid.*

I knelt before her and leaned in to undo first the button and then the zipper of her pants with my teeth. When she was naked, I pushed her backward until her legs hit the bed. She toppled and I followed, crawling up her torso until our breasts were aligned. A quiet moan escaped me at the sensation. Too long, oh, god, it had been too long—I should never have allowed her to keep us apart. She squeezed my hips hard and I slid one thigh between her legs...and then we were rocking together, hands stroking and bodies melding until sweat slicked between us.

"Need you, need you," she gasped, voice breaking as she clutched hard at my shoulders. I knew what she wanted—to get closer, ever closer. It would never be enough.

I kissed her deeply, drinking in her now wordless pleas. "I'm right here," I said against her lips before finally moving down, down the length of her long body, tracing the curves of her breasts as I went. I kept one hand there, twisting and tugging even as her legs cradled my shoulders.

"I love you, Valentine," I whispered, my heart pounding at the beauty of her, spread open before me. "I need you. I need *us*—like this, always."

She started to reply, but I dipped my head, bringing my mouth to her: drinking her in. In this moment, I was the vampire—absorbing her passion into myself, gaining strength from the desire and love and surrender that she offered me freely. She was fire under my tongue, and I clutched at her thigh with my free hand, feeling the world finally slide back into place as she shouted my name in ecstasy.

I stayed with the fitful movements of her body until the tautness eased from her muscles. And then I moved back up, shifting onto my side to press against her while lightly running my fingers through her sweat-dampened hair. Her eyes were still closed, her breathing still shallow. She was exquisite. Love swelled up in me, a solar flare unfurling from the surface of the sun. The influx of emotion made my chest feel tight, and I took a deep, steadying breath.

When Val's eyes finally opened, they were the lightest blue I'd ever seen. She had never looked so soft, so vulnerable, so *mine*. The corners of her mouth twitched, and an answering smile bloomed across my face. "Welcome home, baby," I said, hearing the huskiness in my own voice.

She cradled me close, and I inhaled her scent—spicy and sweet. And then, in a sudden burst of effortless strength, she rolled me beneath her and bent her head to my breasts. The heat of her mouth tore a whimper from my throat, and I arched against her, instantly afire with need. She didn't make me wait, flattening one hand between us, pressing me hard into the mattress as she filled me.

When I called out her name, her mouth was immediately on mine, her free hand cupping my face. She moved confidently, driving me higher with each claiming thrust until I was trembling at the edge of the precipice, poised for flight. Forcing my eyes open, I looked up into her eyes and saw equal parts love and thirst. Without hesitation, I offered my neck, praying that in this moment, she could see past her guilt and fear to my blazing need to nourish her. In all ways.

"Take me. Do. It. Val—"

She thrust deep inside and sheathed her teeth in my neck in one fluid motion. Twin sparks of pleasure and pain fused, igniting my release. My triumphant scream was short and sharp, and I clung to Valentine fiercely as my body shuddered in her arms. Her pull on my blood was only a subtle ache and I welcomed it, loving that only I could sustain her.

After a few moments, she pulled away. I shivered at the loss and leaned into her hand that was tenderly stroking the back of my head. Fatigue had stepped into the vacuum left by my insistent need for her, and I wanted nothing more now than to fall into sleep with her at my side. I cuddled close to her immediately, throwing one arm across her waist and twining our legs together.

"I love you," Val breathed against my hair, rubbing circles against my back. "So much."

"Mine," I said, finding the strength to press one final kiss to the lightly freckled skin of her shoulder. Tonight represented only a small victory in what would be a long battle against Val's inner demons, but I wasn't going to let her pull away from me again. We could do anything, as long as we were together. That was the key. Together, we were stronger than any obstacle.

THE
LETTING GO

Shannon Dargue

It seemed those days the only place Gwen and I could carry on a civil conversation was outside. Without fail, the moment four walls surrounded us, our meetings dissolved into juvenile screaming matches peppered with insults and even the occasional flying dish. So we walked, and although we covered many miles on our city's sidewalks, we hadn't budged an inch on our divorce settlement. More specifically, I refused to give her one. I knew as soon as I signed those papers my wife would take off like a bat out of hell.

I just needed more time.

"This is stupid, Jai. The papers are drawn up, and the legal fees are paid. All you have to do is sign." She stopped and thrust a thick manila envelope and a pen bearing her lawyer's insignia in my face. "You can't force me to stay married to you."

"No, I suppose I can't." I gently pushed the offensive items out of my way and continued walking. "I can, however, try to make my wife see the mistake she's making."

"The mistake *I'm* making?" Gwen was fuming. "*I* did not make a mistake—you did. You fucked someone else! You broke the rules, Jai. We're done."

The truth was, Gwen and I had been legally separated for exactly twelve months, and that was really all the Canadian government required to grant us a no-contest divorce. Well, that and my signature. I couldn't believe it: seven years of my life (for three of which, we were legally wed) were about to disappear because of one indiscretion. That didn't seem fair at all. Nope, Jaidan Elizabeth Marshall would not be signing any divorce papers. I was going to fix everything.

Unfortunately though, my strategy seemed to only further enrage my beautiful, estranged wife. Plus, as she informed me, it could get expensive.

I was grasping at straws, and running low on hope. As we trudged past European delicatessens, vintage record stores, and coffee shops, I turned to face her. Gently placing my hands on her shoulders, I stopped our forward movement and tried to lock eyes with her. Even through her bulky sweater I could tell Gwen had lost weight. Shoulders once square and proud were now frail and birdlike. She looked broken. Mustering every ounce of emotion in my being, I tried to make her understand. "I love you, Gwen." Still, it didn't seem like enough.

Gwen appeared to be deeply engrossed in the pizza-by-the-slice sign above my head. I was certain she was ignoring me until I realized she was struggling to hold back tears. She cleared her throat, attempting to regain her icy composure. Gwen's quivering chin betrayed her.

"Baby, please," I fervently whispered, gripping her tighter. "I know you still love me. It doesn't have to go down like this. I fucked up, but I can make it better. I promise."

Gwen finally met my stare, and as she did so, pent-up tears

spilled over her cheeks and a shuddering sigh racked her tiny frame. "I wish I could believe you, Jai." She began to cry harder.

I didn't know what to do. Yes, I had been the one to make her cry, but for so many years I had held the privileged position of being the one to console her when she was hurting. I wiped her puffy, tear-streaked face with my hands. "We'll be okay." I searched her eyes, and when I thought I saw a glimmer of what used to be, I kissed my wife.

Gwen slapped me so hard, my head spun.

"No, Jai, you can't kiss it and make it all better." I watched her resolve solidify before my eyes. "I need closure. Allow me to have at least that much."

Defeated, I relieved her of that manila envelope and bid her good night.

The following evening, I sat half-drunk in my shitty little apartment with the hateful documents in my lap. I had signed them. Gwen was right; this was entirely my own doing. As I shuffled to the kitchen to retrieve another beer, the phone rang. I waited for the machine to pick up. *"It's Jai, leave a message…"*

A beep, and a click, and there she was. "Jai…it's me… Look I'm—"

I snatched up the receiver. "Gwen, hi." I struggled to sound sober. "I signed the papers."

"Thanks…" She inhaled audibly before continuing on the exhale. "I should never have hit you. That was wrong and I'm so sorry. I feel terrible."

"Nah, it's okay," I lied. I wanted to get off the phone and back to my beer. Listening to her apologize was excruciating. "I deserved it. So when do you want them?"

Gwen left me hanging awkwardly as she mulled over my query.

"Gwen?"

"How about tonight?"

"What? Jesus! What do you need them for now? It's nine thirty." I was already tucking in my shirt and scanning the room for clean socks.

"Please, Jai." I could barely hear her. "I'm done fighting."

"Well, then you'll have to come and get them. I can't drive."

In the twenty minutes I had before my soon-to-be ex-wife showed up, I managed to run the overflowing garbage out to the chute, clear the empties off the table, brush my teeth, and otherwise make myself presentable. The nervous energy created by Gwen's pending arrival had completely burned off the insular haze I'd been cultivating all night.

When the buzzer sounded I froze. At that moment, I fully understood how close I was to being a single woman again. As soon as that damn envelope was back in Gwen's hands, my marriage was as good as dead. Worse still was the cold dread that began to settle in my gut. I didn't believe we could be in a confined space and not verbally rip each other apart—despite her assurances.

The buzzer sounded again, and this time she was really laying on it. "Okay, okay, stop so I can unlock it," I muttered to the wailing rectangle on the wall. She definitely knew how to get my attention. I pressed the appropriate button when she finally let go and waited for her at the door.

I watched, envelope in hand, as Gwen exited the elevator and made her way down the shabby hallway. It was too easy to forget the circumstances surrounding her late-night visit as she approached. In faded jeans and the same ugly, old, grandpa-sweater from yesterday, she was stunning. I desperately wanted to kiss her again, slap or no slap.

"Can I come in?" Gwen asked as she sidled past me into

the apartment, plunking a bottle of wine down on the kitchen counter.

I followed her and eyed the bottle with obvious disdain. "I'm sorry Gwen, but I'm really not up for celebrating." This was over the top, even for her. I was already mentally preparing for the ensuing argument. "Here." I held out the envelope. "By the way, I don't have a corkscrew."

"I brought one—and we aren't celebrating." She fished the chrome implement out of a sweater pocket. "You do have glasses, right?"

I opened the cupboard and revealed two Toronto Maple Leaf mugs. "Then what *are* we doing?" She still hadn't taken the envelope.

Gwen dismissed the question. "Jesus Christ, Jai, this is the most pathetic apartment I've ever seen. Why didn't you take more from the house?" She was moving to the living room.

It was my turn to ignore her. *I didn't take much because I didn't think I'd be in the doghouse this long.* I settled beside her on the couch and privately savored our proximity and the stillness in the room. Accepting the mug she handed me, I fully allowed myself to wallow in that bittersweet moment. It had been so long since we'd been able to just sit quietly together and longer still, since the last bottle of wine we shared. It felt like a first date. I was anxious and full of anticipation. The bubble burst, however, when the legal-sized envelope on the coffee table caught my eye. *Right, she's dumping me.* I struggled to contain the flood of emotion that threatened to drown this peaceful moment.

"You keep playing with it," she sheepishly eyed my fat lip. "Does it hurt?" Reaching out slowly, she tentatively brushed her fingers over my lips.

I shook my head, careful not to pull away from her hand. A

familiar heat rose from within and my pulse quickened. Gripping my chin between thumb and forefinger, Gwen drew my face to hers and gently pressed a feathery kiss to the swollen lip. As I loosened my mouth to grant further access, a tumultuous storm of emotion suddenly ripped through me. I snatched my face away.

"What the hell are you doing?" I demanded, rising to my feet. "This isn't fair."

"Fair? Are you kidding, Jai?" She was clearly flabbergasted. "All things considered…"

"Fuck you, Gwen. I'm tired of this shit, and I'm tired of your games." Hot, angry tears began to flow. "What were you after, one last celebratory fuck? Is that what the wine was for? You haven't let me touch you in a year, and I'm supposed to just roll over *now*?" I tossed the envelope into her lap.

She shot upright and the yellow bundle slid to the floor. She jabbed her pointer finger at me and began her rebuttal, "You don't—"

"Stop it!" I grabbed her outstretched hand. "You've done nothing but drag me over the coals for the last year. I know I hurt you, Gwen, and every day, I wish I could go back and change it all…" I released her now limp arm, "but I can't, and you can't keep punishing me. This war is over. You won, okay? We're divorced."

An extreme weariness washed over her delicate features, taking hold like a dark stain bleeds into pale wood. "So, now what?"

"Let's just drink our wine and try to get along." I went back to the couch and tapped my blue mug against hers. "Cheers," I softly added.

Gwen was visibly confused. This was the first time since we separated that one of our fights simply ran out of steam. I patted the couch, and for the better part of a minute, I watched as she stood motionless, struggling to process the curveball I'd thrown at her.

Choosing a spot about two feet from me, Gwen finally sat. To my surprise, she pulled her feet up and lowered her head to rest in my lap. She closed her eyes and sighed in resignation. "What was her name?"

I began to stroke her hair. "Her name was Amy." Gently tracing a route from her temple to behind her ear, and along her jaw, I felt Gwen's tears seeping through my jeans, finally understanding the depths to which I had wounded her. I waited for her to continue. I knew from experience not to provide information Gwen wasn't ready to process. This was the first time she had requested details.

"So, you met her at work?"

"Yeah." As strange as our present situation was, I was relieved to finally have the opportunity to clear the air. I had at that point entirely given up on mending our marriage. The best I could hope for was honesty.

Gwen asked some more standard questions. Was I planning to leave her before she threw me out? *No.* Did I love Amy? *No.* How many times had I slept with her? *Twice.* She quietly accepted my answers.

"She meant nothing, Gwen." The very instant those words spilled from my mouth, I regretted them. For those words implied that while I was with Amy, Gwen meant even less than nothing. I felt her stiffen. "Fuck—that came out wrong. I don't know...I was just bored I guess. But the last time I was with her, I realized how stupid I had been. It wasn't worth losing you."

Gwen sat up. She wanted to see me answer this final question. "If I hadn't seen the marks, would you have confessed?"

I met her eyes. "Probably not."

She stood up and paced the room. The pretence of calm had been shattered. "You see, Jai? That's why I can't trust you. *That's* why we're done. How do I know you won't pull that shit again?"

I joined her in the center of the room. "Listen to me." I cradled her face in my trembling hands. "When I realized what I had done to you, when I realized how devastated you'd be, I knew I could never tell you." I pressed my forehead to hers, and my hands fell to their natural resting place on her hips. "The guilt was eating me alive, and I could have confessed. It would have been easy to place that burden in your lap, but I couldn't hurt you any more than I already had. I just wanted us to be okay again. Please believe me." I searched her eyes for some indication that I had gotten through.

"It's so hard, Jai." Gwen burrowed into my rumpled shirt as great heaving sobs threatened to shake her apart. I held her tighter, not knowing what else to do, not knowing how to make her stop hurting. In spite of everything, I couldn't help but notice how good she felt.

As she continued to cry into my neck, my fingers slipped under her sweater and found the hem of her T-shirt. After a flicker of uncertainty, I slipped under the thin cotton and delighted in the warmth and softness of Gwen's skin. Gently tracing looping patterns I felt again, for the first time, the shape of her. The shape of my wife. Gwen fell silent.

We stood like this, just testing the water, for many long minutes, until a greater urgency took over. She lifted her face and brushed her lips across my ear. "Mmm...that's nice," she whispered just barely pressing her pelvis to mine. That and the slow movement of her hands on my back assured me that permission had been granted.

I turned my face to meet Gwen's and kissed her. Softly at first,

I kissed the corners of her mouth, and her cheeks, forehead, and eyelids. I kissed every inch of Gwen's face before returning to her mouth for a deep soul kiss. As our tongues met, my roving hands explored the contours of her body and lingered on her breasts. Through the delicate fabric of her bra I could feel her nipples harden as I pinched and worked them between my fingers. Her breathing became ragged and she clutched fistfuls of my short hair. Her simple, primal gesture of need cracked my composure. I kissed her harder, devouring her mouth, seeking to fill the cold void created by her absence.

Steering me toward the hallway, Gwen broke away from my lips to ask if I had a bed. While she spoke, both the sweater and the T-shirt went over her head and onto the floor in one swift motion.

"Yes I do." I released the clasp on her bra. "But I'm afraid we'll pop it." She giggled as I turned us around and lowered her to the couch. I added my shirt to the heap and settled above her with my leg between hers. The sensation of her naked breasts pressed hard against my own caused a flood of wetness in my boxers. I ground my knee into her denim-clad crotch as I nipped, licked, and kissed my way down to her rosy nipples. I relished every sigh and squeal of delight, and dismissed every wiggle and grunt urging me to go faster. If it were up to Gwen, sex would never last longer than ten minutes.

Finally leaving the sweetly scented junction of her neck and shoulder, I continued my descent. She was grinding more urgently now, and I could feel her hot center through my jeans as I took her nipple into my mouth. Alternating between sharp nips and soothing licks, I worked Gwen into a frenzied, frustrated state. It wasn't long before her arm shot between us and made quick work of the buttons and zippers on both pairs of jeans. I had to laugh: same old Gwen. "Has it been a while?"

"Please Jai, I need you."

I had waited so long to hear those words. A wave of joy thrilled through my insides and left me momentarily stunned as I looked down into her eyes. "God, I missed you."

"Mmm-hmm." She wiggled a little. "Pants, Jai..."

She didn't have to tell me twice—okay, three times. Our remaining garments joined the growing pile of laundry on the floor. Being left-handed, I moved to take off my wedding ring so I wouldn't scratch her. I watched her eyes follow the jewelry to the coffee table.

Back in position above her, I kissed the woman who was still legally my wife and nearly swooned when I felt her wetness on my thigh. As my hand snaked down her satiny skin, Gwen's fingers were already between my lips, working my wetness around. "Mmm, baby you feel so good," she cooed into my ear.

From below, Gwen's first two fingers slipped inside and she set a deliberate and measured pace, drawing her fingers nearly all the way out before gliding back into the depths of me. Her thumb kept a constant rhythm on my clit, while urgent, tender little kisses showered my face. The dizzying emotional intensity of this reconnection of our flesh soon set me off balance and turned my arms to mush. I landed face-first in the couch cushion. When Gwen curled her fingers to hit the spot that would send me over the edge, I was suddenly grateful for the sound barrier a face full of couch provided. I held as still as possible as nerve endings deep in my belly began to fire in quick succession, unraveling wave after wave of pleasure. I came hard, riding her hand, smelling the shampoo scent of her hair, feeling her other five fingers clutching my back. I was embarrassed that I came so quickly. "I tried to last baby, I really did."

Gwen wrapped her arms around me and smiled. "Some things never change."

When my heart rate and breathing returned to a normal pace, I began once again the meandering tour of her form with my lips and hands. She bucked her hips and a low growl rose in her throat. She was frustrated.

"Shh..." I kissed around her navel. Despite my best efforts, the understanding that as soon as Gwen was satisfied, I would be just as alone but twice as depressed began to crush my libido. If this was it, I certainly wasn't willing to rush.

I lowered my face to her slightly fuzzy pussy. As I brushed my lips over, around, and through this little swatch of hair, I deeply inhaled her earthy scent. It was that exact moment I realized that she hadn't planned this at all. If Gwen had even *suspected* that she might get laid, she would have shaved. She was both meticulous and predictable. I ran my hand over her knee and, sure enough, encountered soft stubble. I laughed out loud.

Gwen was mortified. "Oh, god, I'm so furry..."

I popped up, kissed a blushing cheek and immediately my desire was rekindled. "No, honey, you're perfect." Without further ado, I slid down her torso and got cozy between her legs.

I tucked my arms under her knees, reached for her hands, and buried my mouth within her folds. Gwen squeezed my fingers so hard it almost hurt. Deeply inhaling her familiar scent, I luxuriated in the perfect softness of these hidden places. I ran my tongue up one side of her engorged clit and down the other, while periodically suckling the hard nub between my lips. Gwen tilted her hips to encourage deeper penetration with my probing tongue. Listening to her pant and moan and call my name nearly sent me over the edge again.

"Baby, please." She released my hands. "I need you inside."

I scooped her ass into my hands, swung her around, and knelt on the floor in front of her. Unceremoniously, I threw her legs over my shoulders and plunged my fingers into her core. My other hand wrapped around her thigh to keep her close to my face. I licked and pumped furiously, while she raked her nails up my back. Gwen breathlessly implored, "Please don't stop, please…" My shoulder burned as I rode the waves of her orgasm and struggled to hold on. A flood of warmth spilled down my arm and Gwen squeezed her legs shut around my ears.

I withdrew my fingers, lowered her feet to the floor, and kissed her stubbly knees. As I did so, she sloppily stroked my head and rubbed my ears. "I missed you too, you know."

I pulled the throw off the back of the couch and wrapped us both in it. As Gwen collected herself in my arms, I couldn't refrain from pointing out the obvious. At the risk of ruining that perfect moment, I said it. "You know, although I can't prove anything, what we just did could technically be considered a breach of our separation agreement." I kissed her shoulder. "And that envelope you've been avoiding all night…"

Laughing softly, Gwen fished my wedding ring off the table and slid it onto my sticky finger. "It's a good thing you're cute."

THE LAST DANCE

Dalia Craig

Summer 1958

She was the most exquisite creature I'd ever seen, gorgeous and incredibly sexy, and she stole my heart in the blink of an eye. From the instant my gaze fell upon her delicate face framed by a sleek cap of auburn hair, and swept past long lashes to drown in her dark amethyst blue eyes, I couldn't stop watching her, or longing to capture those candy-frosted lips in a drugging kiss.

I retreated to a quiet corner with my drink to wait for a chance to introduce myself and to watch her move gracefully around the ballroom chatting and laughing with the guests attending Joy and Adam's first anniversary party. Although she looked outwardly relaxed, I nevertheless detected a hint of wariness in her eyes and a reluctance to stay still for any length of time. I soon arrived at the conclusion that she planned her constant movements specifically to avoid contact with a particular young man who appeared equally determined to shadow her every move.

The ever-moving crowd momentarily obscured my line of vision. When it parted and I could see again, my angel was missing. Devastated by her sudden disappearance, I threaded my way through the guests to the area where I'd last seen her. Having checked the man's position, and satisfied myself that he hadn't left the room, I used what I assumed was her escape route, the open French windows hidden behind long brocade curtains.

Faced with a choice of directions, I followed the gravel path that wound its way between intricate topiary and neatly manicured lawns, toward an ornamental lake where I discovered my instinct had been right. She sat, with her back against a square plinth that supported a large urn, halfway down a flight of wide steps. Below us, the water shimmered like thousands of dark sapphires in the light from the full moon.

She glanced up at the sound of my approach and my heart went out to her when I saw the dampness of tears staining her cheeks. I wanted to reach out and comfort her, to soothe away all her troubles, if only I knew what they were, but I didn't. How could I, when I didn't even know her name let alone her darkest secrets?

"I'm sorry...I didn't mean to disturb you." I began to retreat.

"Don't go." She managed a weak smile and patted the stone beside her in invitation. "I could do with some company and right now I have no desire to return to the house."

I had to agree with her. As Joy's oldest friend and former bridesmaid, I'd felt unable to refuse the invitation, but I'd regretted my decision from the moment that I discovered Joy and Adam were determined to play matchmaker.

Why did happily married people feel it necessary to interfere in the lives of others?

I'd soon managed to escape the clutches of the man they'd invited as my partner, who'd read into his role far more than I was prepared to allow.

Was my angel suffering the same unwanted attention? If so, I'd be more than happy to offer her my protection in return for spending a little time in her company.

"Thank you." I sat down next to her, picking up a hint of her delightful floral perfume as I did so. "I don't think we've met. I'm Dan—Danielle Shawcross."

She took my hand, her delicate fingers curling around mine. "Helena Parkes. I'm Adam's cousin. I recognize you though, from the wedding photos." Her gaze swept over my formal dress and jacket, a concession to the occasion since normally I never wore anything but tailored pantsuits, and she gave a soft laugh. "I must admit you look more at home in proper clothes than in that horrid flouncy thing Joy forced you to wear."

Without warning, she leant across and brushed her lips across mine. My heart raced out of control. I exhaled a long shaky breath: I wanted more than that brief contact. Helena's eyes glittered with amusement as though she read my discomfit. "I'm so glad I moved to Paris just in time to miss all the fun."

"Paris... What an exciting life you must lead there," I teased her gently. How I envied her the freedom to travel—a luxury I couldn't afford on the meager salary paid to junior reporters by our local newspaper. One day, very soon, I vowed, I'd have both the money and qualifications to allow me to work as a freelance writer and journalist. Then I'd have the world at my feet but for the present, I was stuck in this small, narrow-minded town. "I'd love to visit Europe someday." I sighed, thinking not only of Paris, but Rome, Florence, Venice and all the other places that would be on my must see list when I finally realized my dream.

"Yes, I do... You should come soon, I can promise you that you'd have a great time." Her bell-like laughter rang out. "I can hardly wait for Monday, when I can board the plane and leave this dull place behind forever. In Paris I can be who I want, without any constraints, unlike here, and nobody raises an eyebrow if I kiss another woman."

Her casual tone didn't fool me for a minute. Helena betrayed both her youth and naivete by trying to shock me, only she'd picked the wrong person. I didn't shock easily, and kissing other women came naturally to me along with many other activities. I'd happily demonstrate all the ways I wanted to make love to her if she gave me the opportunity. Although I doubted that she would, or that she'd really know what to do if the situation arose. I sighed deeply, picturing Helena naked, reclining on a white satin quilt, ready and waiting for me to teach her everything I knew about love between women. I imagined us making love until, sated from multiple orgasms, we slipped into a deep sleep, then waking to morning sunlight and starting all over again.

Hell! What was I thinking? We were just strangers, thrown together at a party neither of us had wanted to attend. After tonight we would go our separate ways and probably never meet again.

The sounds of music and laughter drifted through the night air, mingling with the gentle swish of water from the nearby fountain.

"Would you like a drink?" Helena produced a champagne bottle from somewhere behind her. "Although I've only got one glass... I wasn't expecting company, maybe we could share?"

"Yes, I'd love some." I smiled, while cursing myself for not having had the foresight to bring something with me. "Or, if you like, I could run back to the house and fetch another glass and maybe some food?"

"Please don't go." Helena placed one hand on my arm, her fingers pressing into my flesh as if she was terrified of being alone. "I'm happy to share if you are, and I'm not hungry."

Neither was I, for food, but Helena was a different matter. If given the chance I'd happily feast upon her delectable body all night.

"Allow me." I took the bottle of *Veuve Clicquot* from her, popped the cork and carefully poured the white froth into the waiting flute. A vision of Helena climaxing onto my tongue sent goose bumps racing up my neck and my pussy clenched with need. I put the bottle down on the step beside me and dug my fingernails into my palms to stop myself from reaching for her there and then.

We shared the whole bottle sip by sip, and then Helena produced another bottle from the same hiding place and by the time we'd finished the second one both of us were in very high spirits.

The unmistakable strains of "Unchained Melody," my favorite song since I'd first heard it sung by Gene Vincent a couple of years earlier, reached my ears. The plaintive notes of the orchestra seemed to linger on the breeze, and the lyrics played in my head calling me to take Helena into my arms. Needing no better excuse to make it happen, I stood and held out my hand. "Will you dance with me?"

"Yes." She moved easily into my arms, her body and mine fitted against each other like two halves of a shell. "I love this song," she murmured dreamily. Her hot breath fanned my neck as we swayed to the hauntingly evocative music barely moving from the spot. Several changes of music later, my hands dropped down to cup her ass and ease her into my body.

Helena reacted positively by grinding her pelvis against mine and I smothered her gasp of pleasure with my lips. She tasted so sweet, like a mixture of honey and champagne.

The pounding beat of my pulse drowned out all other sound. I wanted Helena more than I'd ever wanted anybody in my whole life.

Could I?

Would she?

If I didn't try I would never know, and I only had tonight and tomorrow. Come Monday she'd be gone, out of my life and my arms forever.

I deepened the kiss, my tongue delving into her mouth.

She kissed me back, using her tongue to good effect, proving that I'd misjudged her level of experience by a mile.

"I want you so much," Helena murmured against my lips.

I didn't need a second invitation.

We went back to my place, since she was staying here with Joy and Adam and there was no chance of us sneaking up to her room undiscovered.

What should have been a ten-minute walk across the park took us much longer as every few paces we stopped to kiss and hold each other. We'd hardly got inside my door before Helena grabbed me and thrust me hard against the wall. Her lips devoured mine and her hands tore at my clothes in her effort to get me naked in record time.

"Not here." I grabbed for her hands before I could disgrace myself and take her right there on the hall floor, and then led the way through to the bedroom.

Once there she carried on where she left off. When my dress fell to the floor, I didn't care that she'd ripped it to shreds; I just needed her to touch me, to kiss me and make love to me until she drove all this crazy emotional tension from my system and allowed me to think rationally.

Helena soon dispensed with my bra and panties then turned

around to let me unfasten what seemed like a hundred tiny pearl buttons down the back of her full-skirted cocktail dress. I slipped it off her shoulders and the embroidered silk whispered down into a silvery pool around her feet. I took her hand as she stepped out of it, then I picked it up and draped it carefully across the back of a chair, before removing her delicate underwear.

Jeez, my mouth watered with desire. I wanted to touch and taste every inch of her body. I ran my hands over her luscious curves, lingering awhile to savor her beautiful breasts.

She tried to hook her leg around me but we overbalanced and fell back onto the bed with Helena on top. She trailed hot breathless kisses down my throat, skimmed along my collarbone then traveled lower until she reached my breasts. Her mouth closed over my nipple and I nearly shot into orbit. She circled the sensitive tip a couple of times with her tongue then grazed it with her teeth before giving the other breast the same treatment.

When she tried to kiss her way farther down my body, I called a halt. I rolled her under me, straddled her hips, and sat back on my heels. I trailed my fingers over her silky skin, trying to imprint every inch of her body in my memory yet avoiding the one place I longed to explore.

"Dan! Please...I can't wait I'm..." Her voice cracked as she bucked wildly against me, her fingers crept to her clit in desperate search for relief. "No," I scolded, taking both her hands in mine, pushing them up above her head, and folding her fingers around the brass head rail.

"Open your eyes and look at me." I wanted to make her mine, to pleasure her so that she would remember our first time for the rest of her life.

I returned to my voyage of exploration, touching, kissing and sucking, until I reached my destination, her clit. Helena's lips parted in a breathless gasp of pleasure, and her clit grew into a hard glistening jewel before my eyes. I slipped one finger into her wetness. She was so ready for me; her ragged panting urged me on. I inserted a second finger then slid both of them slowly back and forth.

"Yes!" she cried out, her hips coming off the bed to meet my hand. "Fuck me, baby, I need to come."

"It'll be my pleasure." I grinned and began to move inside her, plunging deep then almost withdrawing, my thumb catching her clit with each inward thrust. Her muscles contracted around my fingers pulling them farther into her pulsating depths. I plunged faster, deeper, harder, until her control shattered.

She looked incredibly beautiful when she came, her lips parted and her eyes deep pools of sensuous desire. I massaged her clit with my thumb, my fingers still pumping deep inside her, prolonging her climax until she stopped gyrating.

I leant forward to kiss her sweet lips; they parted allowing me the freedom of her mouth. I kissed her softly, teasing her with my tongue, willing her to feel the strength of my desire. Her body moved under me, our breasts brushed together, and red-hot arrows speared my core. I sat back again, running my hands down her still trembling body. Helena responded with a contented sigh.

My pussy throbbed. I couldn't hold back much longer. I'd subordinated my own needs for too long already. I began to touch my breasts, alternately flicking and tugging on the nipples until they stood proud and rigid, then I moved lower to part my lips and circle my clit. I dipped one finger into my juices and slicked my clit.

Helena's eyes widened and her breathing faltered. She was clearly as excited by seeing me pleasure myself as I was from doing it. The tip of her tongue snaked out to circle her lips and she moaned softly. I repeated the process, driving my finger deeper into my pussy each time, fucking myself and watching her excitement mount with each stroke of my finger, until the first stirring of my climax developed into an unstoppable tide.

I slid my hands under her ass and lifted her to me, rubbing my engorged clit against her soft mound until I felt her shudder. Her reaction drove me on. I moved faster, slamming against her, seeking the elusive pinnacle of satisfaction.

Our slick bodies moved in unison with one aim and our mouths met in a hot exchange of breath and tongues. "Yes! Fuck me!" Helena's commands were little more than a hoarse whisper against my mouth. Then she raked her fingernails down my back. The searing pain unleashed an instantaneous surge of pressure that moved like a tsunami though my body. I heard her scream my name as her own orgasm hit and a second later, my dam burst.

We clung to each other, just sharing kisses and that intimate, postclimactic oneness, with nothing but our ragged breathing to disturb the silence. Irrationally, I wanted this moment to last forever so we'd never have to say good-bye.

A burst of hysterical laughter bubbled in my throat. This was no story, where a kind fairy godmother arrived at the crucial moment, waved her magic wand and performed a miracle. No way! Come Monday I'd have no option but to stand helplessly by and watch her walk out of my life.

Sunday passed in a blur of hot sex followed by sweet climaxes and short catnaps with the occasional foray into my well-stocked refrigerator for sustenance.

Late in the evening, we sat cross-legged on the rumpled bed, a tray of snacks between us. I broke off a small chunk of rye bread, dipped it into a dish of guacamole, popped a shrimp on top and handed it to Helena. "I wish you didn't have to go tomorrow."

"Me too..." Helena popped the offering into her mouth, chewed and swallowed. "But I have to be back in Paris for a meeting on Wednesday." She licked her fingers, her eyes suddenly alive with a mischievous sparkle. "You could always come with me."

I shook my head. "Sorry, darling. Even if there were a seat available on the plane, which I doubt, I couldn't afford the fare or the other expenses."

"That's no problem; there are always spare seats available for special passengers." Helena shot my argument down in flames. "I'll pay your fare and you wouldn't have to spend a cent on accommodation either; my apartment is plenty big enough for two."

"No... Much as I'd love to come with you, I can't just take an extended vacation without proper notice. I'd lose my job for sure and then there's this place." My rented house was nothing much, a converted two-room shack but it was home, the only one I'd ever had—being in care from the time I was a baby meant I valued my home more than most.

"Are you saying that your job and home are more important than our happiness?" Helena glanced around the bedroom, a frown creasing her brow. "I don't get it. What's so special about living here?"

I shook my head. How could I possibly explain the importance of security to somebody who'd never had to worry about money or a roof over her head?

"Would it make you happier if I paid six months rent for you, and then we can take it from there?"

She had an answer for everything, and this particular one I liked less than all the others combined. "No! I don't fancy being a kept woman."

"Why are you turning me down?" She glared at me. "I

thought we had something special here."

"We have." I hastened to placate her. "I want to come but—"

"Then come... *Come live with me and be my love.*"

"*And we will all the pleasures prove.*" I quoted back. How could I possibly refuse when she asked so nicely?

Helena laughed and clapped her hands. "Wow! You know Marlowe too. That's something else we have in common."

Was it enough? Could I stake everything I held dear on our joint taste in food, music and poetry, plus a couple of nights of hot sex?

"Come on, Dan, where's your sense of adventure."

Hell! She had me there. I could never resist a challenge.

"Will you help me pack?"

"Do you have to ask?" Helena grinned and we leapt off the bed sending our supper flying in our haste to get started.

By agreeing to leave with her, I'd burnt my bridges but what the heck. Saying good-bye would have broken my heart.

Summer 2008

We sat on the patio of our converted farmhouse enjoying a leisurely aperitif, as was our custom on most fine days, shaded from the strong sun by a canopy of purple bougainvillea. The Pyrénées, dividing France from Spain, were little more than a blue haze in the distance.

Strains of "Unchained Melody" drifted out onto the patio from the DVD player inside. Helena smiled and held out her hand. "May I have this dance?"

"Are you sure?"

She nodded, her eyes bright with unshed tears.

I took her hand, helped her to stand, and then wrapped my arms around her. We swayed in time to the music as we'd done so many times in the past, then she gave a ragged sigh and her head rested against my shoulder.

My heart missed a beat. I wasn't ready to say good-bye, it was too soon—it would always be too soon. I helped her back into the chair, stroked her hair, and kissed her lips.

What better way to celebrate fifty years of love and devotion than with a last dance?

ALL IN

Radclyffe

D r. Saxon Sinclair contemplated her scotch rocks and watched the third man in five minutes try to pick up the blonde sitting opposite her at the horseshoe-shaped bar that occupied one corner of the Palace casino lounge. She didn't ordinarily spend her nights in a bar, at least she hadn't for the last five years. But she couldn't sleep and her suite felt claustrophobic. She wondered briefly if the blonde, a fellow trauma surgeon she'd seen at the meeting just that morning, was having similar difficulties. The woman obviously wasn't there to find company for the night, because she quickly dispatched anyone who seemed to be interested. It was possible, Sax supposed, that she and the blonde were both sitting alone at three in the morning for exactly the same reason. A kind of loneliness that went deeper than any physical diversion could assuage.

"No, really, I'd rather just sit here and relax." The blonde's low, musical voice carried surprisingly well despite the cacophony of bells and whistles and constant rumble of voices coming from the gaming floor just beyond the lounge.

Sax narrowed her eyes as a heavyset middle-aged man in an expensive suit put his arm around the blonde's shoulders and leaned down to say something else, crowding her at the same time as he made it difficult for her to move away. Again, she murmured no and shook her head, her expression one of forced pleasantness. Sax imagined the woman was trying to avoid a scene. She knew the man, another surgeon. She had met his wife earlier that week at one of the trauma conference social functions that she hadn't been able to get out of, and remembered him mentioning that his son was a surgical resident somewhere in California. When the blonde signaled no for the third time, Sax felt a surge of anger that brought her to her feet. A woman shouldn't have to say no even once just because she was sitting alone at a bar. She certainly shouldn't have to say no three times. Just as Sax took a step forward, one of the Palace's security guards, recognizable from her understated uniform of dark blazer, white shirt, and dark trousers, as well as by the name tag over her breast pocket and the radio receiver clipped to her ear, appeared as if by magic and tapped the aggressive surgeon on the shoulder. Whatever she said brought a flush to the man's face and he rapidly strode away. As Sax reclaimed her bar stool, she saw the guard murmur a word to the blonde, who fleetingly touched her arm, allowing her fingers to linger for just a moment on the sleeve of the blue blazer. Then the guard, too, disappeared. The exchange had been so brief, Sax doubted anyone would have noticed, but to her, the connection was unmistakable. Her chest tightened and she ached for just a simple touch, just a few seconds of feeling as if she weren't hope-lessly, helplessly adrift.

"Hey," a deep voice said as a hand dropped heavily onto Sax's shoulder. "I called your room and you didn't answer. Listen, I have to go home."

Sax glanced up at her friend and former resident, Quinn Maguire. Some people said they looked alike, but Sax couldn't see it. They both had black hair and blue eyes, sure, but Quinn was an inch or so shorter and more muscular. And more importantly, Quinn always had an air of calm, steady focus about her that Sax rarely managed, especially lately. Right now though, Quinn appeared anything but calm—her cotton button-down collar shirt was rumpled and untucked, hanging out over her jeans. She wore loafers with no socks and had an expression Sax had never seen on her before. Panic.

"What's the matter?" Sax asked.

"Nothing," Quinn exclaimed. "Nothing. Honor called." Quinn's face widened into an enormous grin. "She's in labor. Two weeks early. I gotta go. Sorry to leave you hanging with the panel tomorrow."

"Don't worry about it." Sax stood to give Quinn a quick squeeze on the arm. "Give Honor my love and call me with an update, okay?"

"Yeah. Okay. I will." Quinn turned to go, then looked back, her expression unexpectedly serious. "You're okay, right?"

Sax worked up a smile. "Sure, I'm okay. Jesus, you think I can't get through a twenty-minute presentation without you?"

"That's not what I meant," Quinn said quietly.

"I know what you meant." Sax knew she sounded gruff, but it suddenly felt like she was pushing her words out through ground glass. "Just go, already."

"You'll call me too, with any news, right?"

Sax nodded.

"She's okay, you know," Quinn said.

"Yeah," Sax said roughly. "Sure."

Then Quinn was gone and Sax was alone again. Even the blonde was gone. She sat back down, drained her scotch, and signaled for another. Three weeks. She hadn't heard from Jude in three weeks. It wasn't unusual for her to go days, sometimes a week or even a little longer, without hearing from her, but this was the longest it had ever been. If she knew where she was, or even where to start looking, she would have flown to Iraq four days ago instead of Las Vegas. She knew where Jude had been eleven weeks earlier when she'd started out from Fallujah as one of three embedded journalists with a mobile division of the Second Marines. After that, Jude's emails had been brief and sporadic and absent of any detail. After five years of being married to a documentary filmmaker, Sax recognized Jude's attempts to play down just how bad whatever particular natural disaster or human horror she was investigating really was. She was used to Jude being gone, too, sometimes for weeks at a time. This time it was different. This time she felt their connection, which was always so strong no matter where in the world Jude was, grow thinner and thinner until she feared it had snapped. And as the ties to Jude slid through her fingers like so many infinitesimal grains of sand that she tried so desperately to hold in her closed fists, she watched the world around her fade to a gray unreality, as if she were watching life on the screen of an old black-and-white television. She knew Jude would be pissed at her for losing her grip, so she tried to pretend that life went on. She was at the damn conference, wasn't she?

She rubbed the back of her neck, tired and so damn lost.

"Here, why don't you let me do that?" a husky voice said from behind her as Sax's hand was replaced by two smaller ones.

Sax gripped the rounded edges of the shiny black bar top with both hands, struggling for balance. Her head felt as if a bomb had burst inside it. Her voice came out barely a whisper. "Jude?"

188 BEST LESBIAN ROMANCE 2010

"For your sake, it better be." Jude's breasts pressed against Sax's back as she leaned down and kissed her just below her ear. "Because I'd find out otherwise, and you'd be dead meat, Sinclair."

"How?"

"I saw Quinn grabbing a cab out front. She told me where you were."

Sax hadn't yet glanced behind her, too afraid to discover that she might be hallucinating. Still, when she reached back she grasped a warm hand, rougher than she remembered, but just as strong.

"No, I mean, how are you here?"

"Military transport. I got lucky and there was an extra seat at the last second. It was either get on the plane without calling you, or miss it altogether. I've been traveling about two days."

Finally, Sax swiveled on the seat and faced her lover. Right before she left, Jude had cut her shoulder-length red hair short. It was shaggy and needed a cut now, falling just above her collar in thick waves. She wore a tan T-shirt and faded khaki camos, and even in the low light of the bar, Sax could tell her pale skin had tanned in the unrelenting desert sun. Clearly exhausted, Jude appeared wraithlike, and Sax saw the haunted expression her lover tried to hide with a welcoming smile.

"Hi, baby," Jude Castle said, leaning in between Sax's spread legs and slipping both arms around Sax's neck. She kissed her firmly, but far too briefly, and then leaned back. "I know you hate these conferences, so I thought I'd drop in and distract you."

"Working pretty good so far." Sax rose and slid her arm around Jude's waist. "Let's head upstairs. You look a little tired."

Jude laughed shortly. "I look like hell." She frowned as they started to walk. "You look a little thin, too. And what are you doing up at almost four in the morning?"

"Hoping to get lucky," Sax murmured, kissing Jude's temple.

"Did you?"

"Oh, yeah."

Once upstairs, Sax stripped, lowered the room lights, and turned down the bed while Jude took a quick shower. When Jude walked naked out of the bathroom toweling her hair, Sax's only thought was to get her into bed and hold her. Hold her where she could rest and be safe. Then she registered the scar on Jude's abdomen, immediately assessing in her surgeon's mind the barely healed wound. She was across the room in three long strides.

"What is this?" Sax demanded, unable to keep her fear from translating into anger. A seven-inch-long, angry red ridge wrapped around Jude's left flank just below her ribs "You didn't tell me you'd been injured."

For a second, Jude seemed confused, then she reflexively covered the area with her hand. "God, I'm so tired I forgot about it. It wasn't anything much. Just a glancing—"

Sax spun around and stalked to the far side of the room, which suddenly felt even smaller than it had hours before, when it held only her loneliness. Now there wasn't enough space to contain her rage, but it wasn't Jude she wanted to lash out at. With her back still turned, she snarled, "That's a bullet wound. Do you think I don't know that? Do you think I don't know if the trajectory had been slightly different you'd be dead right now? Jesus Christ, how could you not tell me?"

"I knew you'd worry, and I knew I would be all right," Jude said softly, suddenly right behind Sax. "Baby, you're shaking."

Sax pulled her shoulder away when Jude caressed her. "Don't.

Just…" Her hand was shaking as she swiped the tears that had come out of nowhere too fast for her to stop. Every lost and desolate moment of the last three weeks crashed down on her, and she had a soul-destroying image of what life would be if Jude had not come back. "I'm sorry. I can't…just get in bed. You need to sleep."

Jude wrapped her arms around Sax's body from behind, pressing her breasts to Sax's back and her cheek to Sax's shoulder. "That's not what I need. That's not what I traveled around the world for. Turn around."

Sax had never been able to say no to Jude, and she couldn't now either. But she didn't want her to see what must be in her eyes. Desperation, and devastation. Not quite looking at her, Sax grasped Jude's hand and led her to the bed. Then she drew her down and pulled the covers to their waists as they faced each other. Stroking wet strands of red hair back from Jude's cheek, she whispered, "Close your eyes. Sleep will be good for you."

"When I first got…hurt," Jude said, her eyes wide and never leaving Sax's, "the first thing I thought was that I was still alive, and there were others near me who weren't. I was glad, glad it was them and not me, and part of me knew that was wrong."

"No," Sax said, the agony of imagining Jude wounded making her voice sound harsh. "There is no such thing as justice in war. You were lucky, and it's okay to be glad."

"And then for a while I didn't have time to think at all." As she went on, Jude caressed Sax's face and Sax gently stroked Jude's body, taking care not to disturb the freshly healed wound. "When I got my turn with the medic and he was stitching me up, I thought of all the times I'd filmed you doing the same thing. Saving lives. I missed you so much right then."

"I would've come over there, if I'd known you were hurt."

Jude smiled and traced her fingertips over Sax's mouth. "I

know. But I really wasn't in danger. After a few days, I wasn't even sore. It just looks bad."

"You forget who I am," Sax grumbled, capturing Jude's hand and rubbing it against her cheek. "Don't try to snow me."

"Baby, I'll never forget who you are." Jude shifted closer, pressing her breasts to Sax's and tilting her hips until their lower bodies melded. "I'm sorry you were scared."

"Terrified," Sax said hoarsely.

"When it was bad," Jude whispered, "worse than bad, and I felt things inside of me breaking..."

Sax cradled Jude's face against her throat, stroking her hair. "It's okay, baby. It's okay."

"I knew," Jude said, her mouth against Sax's skin, "you'd heal me." She tilted her face up, trembling in Sax's arms. "Please, baby. I don't need sleep. I don't need food. I don't even need you to take the nightmares away. It was hot, always so hot, and I'm still cold. I need you to make me feel again."

"I need you in order to live," Sax murmured, gently pushing Jude onto her back. She settled her hips between Jude's legs and held her body above her, braced on her forearms. "Are you sure you're not hurting too much?"

"I need you." Jude wrapped her legs around the back of Sax's thighs, lifting into her, pressing as tightly as she could. "Inside me. It's all I've been able to think about since I left there."

Sax *wanted* to be inside her—inside her body, inside her heart, inside her soul. She wanted to bleed into her, until their very cells were indistinguishable. She wanted her so badly she was afraid. Tenderly, carefully, she spread her fingers through Jude's tangle of still strangely short hair and kissed her eyelids, her temples, the corners of her mouth. Jude smelled fresh and clean from the shower, her skin faintly roughened from the wind and sun. Sax traced the edge of Jude's jaw with the tip of her tongue, then trailed kisses down her neck. The stress of holding back the flash fire burning through her, coupled with her anxiety over going too fast, sent her already on-the-edge nervous system into overdrive. She struggled for breath as her body quivered uncontrollably.

"Oh, baby," Jude murmured, caressing Sax's back and ass with long, urgent strokes. "Oh, baby, don't hold back. You need me. And god, I love that you do." She knew just how to break Sax's control, and as she gripped Sax tighter with her legs, she bit down hard on the thick muscle that slanted from Sax's neck to her shoulder.

"God!" Sax reared her head back and tried to pull away. "You don't know what I'll do. I'll hurt you!"

"No, you won't," Jude said fiercely, tears streaking her cheeks. "You can't. Please, please, help me!"

Jude's tears did what nothing else could. They penetrated the shroud of desperation and fear that had clouded Sax's mind and heart for weeks. She saw her lover clearly, saw her need, saw her vulnerability. And reflected in her lover's eyes, she saw herself—slowly dying for want of this woman. Rocking back on her knees, Sax placed her palm between Jude's breasts and spread her fingers, bracing herself as she brought her other arm between Jude's legs and entered her. She knew this woman, this body, this flesh that welcomed her, and she buried herself there. Jude bucked off the bed, her voice a strangled scream, and Sax held her down as she thrust into her.

"You feel me?" Sax rasped, the muscles in her chest and arms straining as she held herself in check even as she pushed deeper. She rolled her thumb over Jude's clitoris until it hardened. "Can you?"

"Yes," Jude cried, her heels digging into Sax's legs as she forced herself harder against Sax's hand. "Deeper, please, deeper.

Oh, god."

Sweat dripped from Sax's face onto Jude's, mixing with her lover's tears, as she filled her again and again. Jude strained and writhed beneath her, struggling to climax. Her head whipped from side to side, her breath torn from her in strangled moans.

Jude's eyes opened wide, her face a mask of agonized need. "I can't. Oh, god, I can't feel...I can't..."

Instantly, Sax stilled, panting to pull air into lungs that burned. Her arms trembled, her stomach was rigid with her own need for release, but she forced her voice to be quiet and calm. "It's okay. Just breathe for a second. Breathe, baby."

Jude gasped for breath and Sax stretched out beside her, cradling her face against her chest. She stroked her sweat-soaked hair. "It's okay, baby."

"I need... Oh, god, I feel numb. I can't and I need..."

Jude's heart pounded against Sax's breast, erratic and urgent. Sax cupped Jude's face and brushed her thumb over Jude's mouth. "Look at me. Look at me, baby."

When Jude focused on her, Sax whispered, "Stay with me. Stay right here with me." Then she reached down and began to stroke her. When Jude whimpered and thrust against her hand, Sax kissed her and whispered again, "Look at me. Just look at me and know I love you more than life."

"I need you to make me come," Jude moaned, clinging to Sax's shoulders, her back arching with the growing pressure. "Need you. Need you so much."

"I'm here." Sax felt the rapid pulsations in the swollen flesh beneath her fingers that signaled Jude's gathering climax. She bore down on Jude's clitoris, giving her the short, firm strokes she knew she needed to push her over the edge.

Jude closed her eyes, crying out her pleasure, and then Sax filled her again. Straddling Jude's thigh, she pushed into her, stroke after deep stroke. Sax came swiftly with her clitoris crushed to Jude's hard body, and Jude came a second time and then a third. Sax didn't stop until her strength gave out and she collapsed into Jude's arms.

"You okay?" Sax gasped, unable to raise her head from Jude's shoulder. She felt Jude weakly caress her neck.

"I will be," Jude murmured. "I'm here with you. I'm home."

ABOUT THE AUTHORS

KRIS ADAMS works in the book publishing industry. She got her start in the eighties penning erotic fantasies starring her friends and their favorite pop stars. Her work has appeared in *Best Women's Erotica 2009*.

JACQUELINE APPLEBEE (www.writing-in-shadows.co.uk) is a black British bisexual woman who breaks down barriers with smut. Jacqueline's stories have appeared in *Iridescence: Sensuous Shades of Lesbian Erotica*, *Best Lesbian Erotica 2008*, *Ultimate Lesbian Erotica 2008* and *2009* and *Best Women's Erotica 2008* and *2009*.

CHEYENNE BLUE's (www.cheyenneblue.com) erotica has appeared in *Mammoth Best New Erotica*, *Best Women's Erotica*, *Best Lesbian Love Stories*, *Best Lesbian Erotica*, *Foreign Affairs: Erotic Travel Tales*, *Rode Hard, Put Away Wet: Lesbian Cowboy Erotica* and *After Midnight*.

DALIA CRAIG (www.daliacraig.co.uk) lives in an isolated area of northern Scotland and grew up surrounded by books. She has recently developed an interest in lesbian erotic romance and has published a number of short stories.

ANDREA DALE's (www.cyvarwydd.com) stories have appeared in *Playing With Fire, Do Not Disturb: Hotel Sex Stories, Afternoon Delight: Erotica for Couples* and *The Mammoth Book of the Kama Sutra*, among others. With coauthors, she has penned the novels *A Little Night Music* and *Cat Scratch Fever*.

SHANNON DARGUE is a carpenter living in Calgary, Alberta, with her partner of seven years and their twelve-year-old daughter. Her work can be found in *Best Lesbian Romance 2009*.

SACCHI GREEN's stories have appeared in many collections, including *Best Lesbian Erotica, Best Women's Erotica, Best Lesbian Romance* and *Penthouse*. With Rakelle Valencia, she has coedited three lesbian erotica anthologies: *Rode Hard, Put Away Wet*; *Hard Road, Easy Riding*; and *Lipstick on Her Collar*. She is also the editor of the recent anthology *Girl Crazy*.

SOMMER MARSDEN's (SmutGirl.blogspot.com) work has appeared in *I Is for Indecent, J Is for Jealousy, L Is for Leather, Spank Me, Tie Me Up, Whip Me, Ultimate Lesbian Erotica 2008, Love at First Sting, Open for Business, Tasting Her, Hurts So Good, Seduce Me, Best Women's Erotica 2009, Seduction, Lust at First Bite* and *Yes, Sir*.

ANNA MEADOWS's work has appeared in *Circuit West* and the online magazine Angelingo. She volunteers for ONE National Gay and Lesbian Archives, where she writes for their LGBT history timeline.

EVAN MORA is a recovering corporate banker living in Toronto whose works can be found in *Best Lesbian Erotica 2009*, *Best Lesbian Romance 2009* and *Where the Girls Are.*

ERIN O'RIORDAN (www.aeess.com) enjoys reading and writing in the many genres of romantic and erotic literature. She has short stories appearing in Oysters & Chocolate and Tassels & Tales. Her erotic romance novel, *Beltane*, was published in 2008.

HANNAH QUINN lives in Bristol, the United Kingdom, with her partner and their growing family of rescue cats. She is new to writing but loves to write short fiction about women, love, loss and pleasure. She is part of a growing community of local writers and artists whose power and passion inspire her.

PAMELA SMILEY gathered the life stories of Korean women while studying feminist theory and the body during a Fulbright to Ewha Woman's University in Seoul, Korea. Creative writing seemed the only way to capture the richness and suggestiveness of these women's experiences.

NELL STARK AND TRINITY TAM (www.everafter.com) blame Radclyffe for infecting them with vampirism. Their collaboration *everafter*, the first paranormal romance novel in a five-book series, was published in 2009.

RENÉE STRIDER is a Canadian living in Canada. Some of her stories can be found in *Erotic Interludes 2–5*, *Fantasy*, *Read These Lips*, *Best Lesbian Love Stories: Summer Flings*, *Toe to Toe* and *Girl Crazy.*

ABOUT
THE EDITOR

R ADCLYFFE (www.radfic.com) is a retired surgeon and full-time award-winning author-publisher with more than thirty novels and anthologies in print. Seven of her works have been Lambda Literary Award finalists including the Lambda Literary Award winners *Erotic Interludes 2: Stolen Moments,* edited with Stacia Seaman, *In Deep Waters 2: Cruising the Strip*, and the romance *Distant Shores, Silent Thunder.* In addition to editing the current volume and *Best Lesbian Romance 2009* (Cleis Press), she has edited *Erotic Interludes* 2–5 and *Romantic Interludes 1 and 2* with Stacia Seaman (Bold Strokes Books), and two solo erotica collections (*Change of Pace* and *Radical Encounters*), has selections in multiple anthologies including *Best Lesbian Erotica 2006, '07, '08,* and *'09; First Timers, After Midnight, Caught Looking: Erotic Tales of Voyeurs and Exhibitionists, Ultimate Undies: Erotic Stories About Lingerie and Underwear, Naughty Spanking Stories 2, Hide and Seek, A Is for Amour, H Is for Hardcore, L Is for Leather, Rubber Sex, Tasting Him,* and *Lesbian Cowboys: Erotic Adventures*. She is the recipient of the 2003 and 2004 Alice B. Readers' award for her body of work and is also the president of Bold Strokes Books, one of the world's largest independent LGBTQ publishing companies.